Rosalyn Chissick is a novelist, poet and journalist; her work has been published in national newspapers and magazines including the *Independent on Sunday*, *Guardian*, *The Sunday Times*, *Elle* and *New Woman*. She has won prizes for extracts from this novel, including the 1995 Armagh Writers' International Short Story Award and the 1996 Waterstones and Terence Higgins Trust Short Story Competition (published in *It Must Be Love*, Penguin Books, 1997). She lives in Wiltshire.

Catching Shellfish between the Tides

Rosalyn Chissick

SCEPTRE

The story told in Colours is borrowed from a Chinese folk tale.

Copyright © 1998 by Rosalyn Chissick

First published in hardback in 1998 by Hodder and Stoughton
First published in paperback in 1998 by Hodder and Stoughton
A division of Hodder Headline PLC
A Sceptre Book

10 9 8 7 6 5 4 3 2

British Library Cataloguing in Publication Data

Chissick, Rosalyn
  Catching shellfish between the tides
  I. Title
  823.9'14 [F]

  ISBN 0 340 70775 5

Typeset by Palimpsest Book Production Limited,
Polmont, Stirlingshire
Printed and bound in Great Britain by
Mackays of Chatham PLC, Chatham, Kent

Hodder and Stoughton
A division of Hodder Headline PLC
338 Euston Road
London NW1 3BH

for Tara

With thanks to my friends, especially Alyson Hallett, Christine Valentine, Elisabeth Winkler, Mercedes Catton, Michael Chissick, Murray Groves, Nick Morgan and Sally Adams.

Contents

1. Bone

In the first light of morning, the boat is a dark whale. On the jetty there are people and boxes, bags, trunks, sacks. A child who cannot keep up lies on the concrete.

You going on the boat?

A tall man in black denim, clutching a little suitcase. He looks like he has slept in his clothes. His skin is too big for him, puckering and wrinkling all over the place.

Yes.

Leaving for good?

Yes, Magda says, for better. Forever.

It's going to be a long journey. Be glad to have some company.

The sea shimmers. Purple and perfectly smooth.

I want to be on my own, she says.

He says: it was never my plan to take aloneness away

from you, then he threads away. He has a slight limp, his whole body tilted to the left, arms at odd angles.

Wads of newspaper blow around her ankles. She listens to the faraway sound of traffic and music drifting from a passenger's radio.

The boat pulls out at dawn. Magda enjoys the feeling of floating, standing on the deck, watching the brown hunched land become fist-sized, then speck-sized, then a dirty jagged memory.

Birds make patterns in the sky. She throws a bottle in the water and it sinks out of sight.

The weather changes and leaves its colours on her skin. Sitting in a deckchair, she tries to catch the moment when day becomes night.

There are the weathered floor boards of the deck, the sea, the sky and bottles in corners. Birds that swim. Men who tell jokes over red wine.

One night, they sit as a big family around a seventy-foot oak table. There is a swan carved out of ice on a river of scarlet petals. They watch it melt in pools.

A woman puts a black rose between her teeth, twists her arms and dances on the table, heels spiking braille into cloth. Her husband takes a picture.

In the smoky room a few people move slowly on the dance floor. Magda's hair sweats down her back. She opens the door to let a cool breeze float through. The man with a limp takes a drag on his cigarette, the ash-glow lights his face and he is beautiful. He exhales with a long lazy breath and she touches his face.

The stars are ragged in a mottled gas-blue sky. They stand on the deck listening to the moan of the wind and she reaches for him. His laughter runs across the back of her neck. His damp T-shirt is soft against her face. He smells of sea water and wet leaves. They push against each other and his slow warmth eases through her, fingers snaking behind her neck and pulling her down.

Dress around her hips, the cry of birds hanging in the air. His legs are covered with fine hairs. The one with a limp shivers. Warm arms, warm chest. She pulls him hard into her.

The morning is crisp and he turns his collar up. Walking arm in arm, talking in each other's faces.

I'm going to Sicily, he says.

The sun peeks in shades of orange.

She says: I need to go further than that.

She can go with him. From the first moment on the quay. From the second when he sloped away, one arm twisted out behind him, it was always an option.

He says: come with me. Some nights you might like to pull up a chair beside me and tell me something small. And I might like to listen or I might not. But I'll be

warm and real and alive. And that might be everything
we need.

He puts his arms around her, pulling her to him.

I won't ask you to stay, he says, and you won't have to
ask to leave.

He is a man with an edge. Like a rock or an ice cube.
She can trace his outline with her finger.

There's nothing I need that I can't get for myself, he says.
Nothing I want from you that you won't want to give.

His words are like spinning balls of light. But she wants
to be alone.

Two months later, in a small whitewashed room in Crete,
Magda is sick in an enamel sink. Pregnant. Raw ragged
sounds fill the empty room. Her tears are too big to be
held in her hands.

She craves salt. The smell of fresh fish from the market fills her nose and mouth until she cannot stop herself running towards it. Calamari, Sea Bass, Red Mullet.
Tails flapping, scales rippling, blue, pink, mother-of-pearl,
black. Silver-brown innards slop in plastic buckets.

She eats so fast she can barely taste. Licking bones
until they shine. Fish in her body feeding another body
beginning to grow. Wheel of death and life. As impossible
to separate as layers of skin.

She gets a job in a restaurant, swirling pale fish in

bread crumbs and egg, watching them spit and flop in hot oil. Emptying bins filled with old newspapers and bones. Wiping greasy counters. Counting greasy coins. It is not in her nature to save and yet the coins become notes in an elastic band in a biscuit tin.

On a pink Greek beach, Magda is a puddle shivering in the midday heat. To dislodge the baby, she drinks tumblers of gin, takes scalding baths, eats aspirins and yellow berries the coarse-faced landlady warns her to avoid. And still, inside its sac, the child's tiny arms, purple veins and translucent head keep growing.

God, help me, please. Magda is on her knees. I'll never ask for anything again. Let my baby die in my belly.

In the hospital where no one knows her name, Magda rises and falls with pain and sweat, while blood and green water pour from her. Her flesh tears and a nurse with hair like black candy floss says: girlbaby.

There she is, all sticky and wizened. Skin so thin Magda can count her ribs and veins.

Magda thinks: to be a mother, I must be:
living
bright
beautiful
big-breasted
wide-smiling.

But she has no words for how she feels. Just the glass of water in her hand. The thin stained sheet over her body. The yellow light on the open book where she has written: I have a dream that I am a mother on the worst night of all.

Naomi, Carla, Susan, Bethan, Riana, Melanie, Lesley, Claire. Magda calls her baby Missing because, like everything else, she knows she will lose her.

Greek nurse says: no husband – and her lips are a thin tangerine line.

Greek doctor says: no husband – and his hands flutter over her belly and stay too low too long.

He tells her he has an apartment in Athens, a hip flask of ouzo, three gold teeth and a wife running a pension on one of the islands. There is a waterfall in his courtyard. It sounds like china breaking over and over. The scent of wax polish on marble floors.

She goes with him because he asks her to.

Each night he comes back from the hospital smelling of antiseptic. The dark hairs on his back matted like fur. He wants her then. The marble floor makes her shiver.

He sings in the shower. Triumphant songs that bounce off the walls and choke the apartment until she hangs her head out of the bedroom window, fills herself with air.

He drinks wine in his dressing gown. She cooks his meat

lightly. Serves it with aubergines and olives. Watches him eat, dripping oil on to his chest. The sound of him chewing, picking pieces from his teeth, wiping them on his napkin.

He likes her to massage his feet with almond oil. Fingers slipping between his toes, over his ankles, up to his shins. His belly rising and falling like a balloon.

Magda wakes to the sound of the doctor cleaning his teeth in the en suite bathroom. His mouth is filled with paste and saliva. She buries her head under the sheet.

He comes back into the bedroom with a towel wrapped around his waist.

Have breakfast with me.

She nods. Puts on jeans and a shirt from a pile lying by the bed.

Missing starts to cry.

Oh God. Magda fumbles with the buttons of her shirt and one comes off in her hand.

Yoghurt, cold toast, thick dark coffee. Missing lying in her lap. The doctor reading the paper and the post.

The bang of the door then silence. She drinks weak tea with honey and eats an apple. Missing drinks, sleeps, cries, makes bubbles with her mouth, wriggling worms with fingers and toes.

Magda thinks: I made her. Every soft and shiny inch of her. Does that make her mine?

Magda and the doctor meet in a restaurant with paper tablecloths. Wild flowers wilt in empty wine bottles.

He says: are you happy?

She picks wax from the bottle neck; the cloth blows against her bare legs.

Sometimes, yes.

They drink sangria, thick with fruit. Eat tsatsiki – she no longer has the stomach for fish – and hard white rolls.

She looks in the pram and says: Missing looks beautiful when she is sleeping. Takes the doctor's hand in hers.

Walking by the sea, the wheels of Missing's pram bump over pebbles and cans. Missing is filthy. Her front covered with a sour yellow froth.

Magda runs water in the wash basin, tests it with her elbow. At first Missing struggles, flails her arms. Then she relaxes, pushing her toes against the sides of the sink. Her body is creased. Round and fat. Magda soaps her, fingers slipping, splashing water over slithery skin.

The water is cooling. So easy to hold her under.

Magda swaddles Missing in a towel; cold and wet. Makes a cup of coffee to clear her head, but it is bitter and hard to swallow.

2. Orange

The doctor wears a white shirt and trousers the colour of the sky after it has rained. He stands in the bedroom doorway with a bunch of orange flowers in one hand (wrapped up in tissue paper and string) and a newspaper in the other. His keys jingle in his fingers and the sound is so loud and so near Magda covers her ears with her hands.

The doctor is a big man. Tall, broad, long-legged. It does not take him long to cross the room to sit beside her on the bed. He kisses her and his big, wide mouth covers hers completely.

The baby is lying in Magda's arms. Bundled up in white so only a half moon of face is visible. He strokes her cheek. Cold. He holds a still-damp curl of her hair between his thumb and forefinger and, as he does, he breathes in a stillness he knows as intimately as his own smell.

No, he says. No.

He stands because he can't stay sitting down. He walks towards the window because that's where his legs take him. He presses his forehead against the glass because it feels solid.

In the kitchen, he pours a glass of ouzo. Swallows. Pours another. Follows the line of fire from mouth to throat. Walks around the room like an animal newly caged.

Magda's head is a box. In it there is the line of a song: catch me, catch me, catch me. Over and over. It fills all the space in her head and when it does not – when a chink appears and the chink is the beginning of a chasm and the chasm has no bottom and no walls – she counts the words. Then she counts the letters, then the letters and the words. Catch me, catch me, catch me.

The bedspread swirls and loops under her fingers. Tracing, retracing until without wanting to call him, without wanting him at all, there is just the doctor's name:

Pavlos.

Magda is shouting with her whole voice.

She holds the baby out to him like something she has

found. Like she expects him to do something with it. But they are both scared.

No, he says. No.

Magda's eyes are blue. Her fingers are mauve. The baby is a hundred blues and mauves in between.

No, he says. No.

The bundle is light in his hands. Light and so heavy he falls to his knees with the effort of not dropping it.

I don't want to know what happened, he says, or how or why. Don't speak of it, he says. Don't speak of it now or at any time in the future.

When he stands he is a big man again, a doctor.

I'll say she died of natural causes.

The woman rocking back and forth like a devotee at prayer has no use for his words. He knows that. He says them for himself.

I will cover it up. I will make it all right.

There is a small shaded area at the side of the house. Flowers are planted there and a tree with branches like green fingers. They prod the air, make small sharp circles when the wind is all around.

The doctor makes a hole in the ground and puts the bundle inside: white wool blanket, pale blue baby. He looks at her in the hole. Red earth, grey and black stones. He cannot cover her with more of the same. Not yet. Stands looking. Feeling his heart inside his body. A clock that is ticking too fast.

The woman that stands behind him now is barely a woman at all. Walking from the bed to the door, through the lounge and out into the courtyard, there was no part of her choosing to move and only the smallest part of her aware that she was moving. Floating almost. Gliding towards: blue baby in a red-brown hole, white blanket mirroring the white of the clouds and the circular jets of the fountain as they collide with the air.

She stands behind the doctor so that her view is mainly of his back: wet shirt clinging to shoulders, moulded to the line of bumpy round bones running down the centre of his back.

The air is still. So still a single leaf falling from the tree captures the attention of them both. It lies on the ground, sides curling upwards.

She murdered her baby, held her head under a sink of warm water and watched her turn the palest of blues. Dot of ink in a glass of milk blue.

He lifts the first spade full of earth and drops it into the hole. It covers the baby almost entirely. It is a relief. After that, he can almost convince himself that what he is burying is not important.

Such a little baby. So light, she held her with one hand, dried her on a big white towel. Wrapped her in yards of crocheted wool, laid her in the bed and watched her breathless, dreamless sleep.

Magda is crying. Tears that are dry and soundless. Locked up inside her body. She stays standing where she is long after the doctor has gone, long after the sky has grown dark and hidden everything.

She sleeps for four days, holding to her belly a square, flat pillow. It smells of her. The deepest places inside her. It stores her fitful dreams and the shapeless words she throws out. It is part of her. And as separate as the bricks of the house.

On the fifth morning she buries it, along with most of her hair – cut off in fat ribbons with the scissors the doctor uses to trim his nails. Her head feels spiky now, sharp and rough. She touches it all the time. Imagines her head is covered with pins.

He does not want her any more. To touch her body is to touch something that has rotted and died yet wears the bright clothes of the living. He is not fooled. In bed at night a deep dry river lies between them, stranding them on opposite banks. When he wakes to find a leg or arm encircling his former lover, he recoils.

She does not notice. Hunched in on herself, Magda is an island. The dry river is a moat, cutting her off on all sides.

3. Tattoo of the moon

Magda opens the bedroom curtains. Sees the live green of an arching tree, the skim of a bird's wing and the way the air settles itself afterwards, as if the bird has never been.

She sits that way for a while, on the edge of the bed, looking out at a square of green and grey-blue. Then she packs a small bag.

In the courtyard, she stands and feels the sun outside and inside her body as if there is no body at all. The breaking china sound of the fountain. Orange flowers in a pot on a mound of red earth. She picks up a stone and puts it in her pocket. So hot it could burn a hole.

Magda walks and the sun sticks her dress to her body like a second skin. She walks, one foot in front of the other, as if she knows where she is going, as if there is a place waiting for her. When night falls and she finds herself standing outside the doctor's house, she goes back inside.

The next day, she sets off again. First one foot, then the other. Moving forward. That night she sleeps in the doctor's bed. Tired limbs falling in the river between.

Nine days, nine times she picks up her bag and walks with it. On the tenth day, as she is standing on a street corner, the sky splits. Big trees blow down. So many leaves, yellow, green and brown mashed together in a splash painting of a storm.

Outside, there is so much light it makes her squint and then so much dark, it makes her close her eyes to see the dancing colours.

She is looking in the window of a bookshop and hiding from the storm, when—

Wait for me.

A man is running up behind her. The thump of his boots on the thinly-covered concrete. Thump wait, thump for, thump me. As if she is going to leave him behind.

A tall man in black denim, his whole body tilted to the left.

At last, he says. I've found you, he says. I haven't been able to forget you since the night on the boat.

Above her the roof leaks a steady drip of oily water down

the blue front of her blue dress. She stands there hiding and being seen and the leak becomes a hole through which she can see the layers of cloud in the sky and the drip drip drip becomes a sea which almost covers her.

She shivers and feels hot because he is looking at her and she is looking at him and the water keeps falling on their bodies and the sea which is his face becomes the sea in which they stand. There is nothing else.

They hide together in a bar with Formica tables and flowers in glass jars – red, white and pink. His hair is black, silver stars in his ears.

And she drips on the parquet floor and sips coffee, feels it burn. Watches him with a cake, bite down and bite again, wiping his sticky fingers and the smudged corners of his mouth with a serviette. She can taste the sweetness on the hard red paper.

At the next table, a woman in a cardigan and sling-back shoes eats baklava. She peels it out of its crinkly white jacket, hunches over her plate, eats, sips her tea, sighs, picks the last crumbs off her plate with spittle fingers.

So many moving mouths.

She murdered her baby because there was a wind blowing in her head and she couldn't hold onto her thoughts. She wanted to walk and keep walking. Twenty years old. Silver bangles up to her elbows and on her left shoulder a tattoo of the moon.

The rain does not stop. All over, bigger and bigger holes are appearing. Flakes of concrete and peeling wall sit on shoes and bags. Some people go home. Others pretend they haven't noticed and that they are not afraid. They buy beers for strangers, slamming their coins on the dusty counter. They ask for clean ashtrays and dishes of salted nuts.

Waiters weave their way through debris to bring customers their orders. Children play hide and seek, running up and down.

Magda thinks: he must never know about Missing. I will never tell.

Be careful. A pink mum in a pink dress cries out. You might fall.
Mightfallmightfallmightfall.

4. Catching shellfish between the tides

Slipping and sliding with sand, she scoops shellfish between her fingers. They wriggle in a jam jar.

Sinking sun, lipstick-coloured sky. If she was alone here, she would stay on the beach, light a driftwood fire, boil her pink and grey booty. Eat it too hot. But he waits in the beach hut with egg-shell walls and other people's footprints on the bath mat. Waits with red wine, bread and oranges.

The sand is flour between her toes. She stretches, holds out her arms to feel the air in places tight and shut — fingers, wrists, the skin between her shoulders. She spins, holding out her dress.

Now he walks up the beach, trousers rolled around his

ankles, kicking at the sea through the spray. They feed the sea gulls from his bread-filled pockets. Their wings flap so close to their faces they have to shut their eyes. The birds call for more and he says, there is no more. Lagging behind, she rummages in her pockets, trying to find more than a handful of crumbs, fluff balls and grit.

Shellfish rattle in a pan over a Calor gas flame. He butters bread, pours wine, rubs aloe vera lotion along her back – sand and cool, scratch and stroke. So much on so little skin.

They sit on the balcony, squeezed around a tiny round table. The wind battles the candles and tangles her hair. The shellfish flesh is like moss but sweeter.

He says, this is as good as it gets.

She wanted to eat on the beach and spin. It gets better than this, she doesn't know how much, but it does.

She says, how can you be sure? Because it is better than saying you're wrong.

He says, I just know, and refills his glass.

On the rented bed in the rented room, they get as close as they can without melting. They ride inside the flames but afterwards they pull back from each other, light cigarettes, swig mineral water, have separate dreams.

Her dreams have soft purple hearts and liquid centres. She

is always outside the centre. If she sits in the centre of her life, what will she do for edges? What will the edges do? Change is alway possible, but she's not always sure she wants it. Stuck. That has a comforting, marble-in-her-palm feel about it.

Wake up.

His knees are moulded into her back.

You were talking in your sleep. Losing your marbles.

What?

You were talking about losing your marbles.

I was dreaming about change.

He was dreaming about concrete fish at the bottom of the sea with mercury bellies. Dreaming that he dived in and brought them to the surface, one by one. Dreaming he was a rescuer, against the odds.

She says, hero.

He says, given the chance. Stands smug in coffee-coloured boxer shorts and a three-day tan. Pale brown man. Her brown man pales.

Today, long round body buried in sand, she is a heavy woman. She starfish lies, sharp splinters of shell behind her knees. Large clouds shift across the sky; heads, cats and misshapen moons. She feels his hands walling the sand and thudding around her.

He asks, how does it feel to be buried alive?

She says, it's better than being buried dead.

He asks, is it? because he thinks a lot about death.

She is a white whale in a sand sea, a green-haired mermaid in a stiff and gritty bodice.

She says, it is hard to move. The sand squeezes my ribs with every breath.

He is so close he is blocking the sun, a long silhouette with spiked hair and a dark featureless face. A threadbare wool jumper sags around his thin arms.

He says, stop breathing.

His voice comes from his stomach and tugs at hers.

Stop breathing.

This time it is a request.

Grey sky, all this brilliant yellow, her shoes and rucksack lying on the beach like dead birds, the ache, the faint nauseous smell of salt and silence.

The beach is deserted.

She holds her breath and in the sand hole feels cold on her skin. She stops counting the seconds, but keeps looking at him, staring at her. The white skin of his face, dark purple eyes, a fringe of black lashes.

She no longer knows where the division is between her breasts and the sand, her belly and the sand. She is a dot, a yellow dot.

He says, you are violet-coloured. He says, the tide is coming in.

Now breath burns in her. She doesn't move but trembles. He scrapes the sand off her body with care. The air seems to caress her. Time has stopped. They walk back along the sand in silence.

Under a pale sky she says, half dead, half alive. Most of life is like this. If I knew what I wanted I would go after it. Hunt it down in forests, under the sea, in the sky. Find it, take it.

She says, I would be one quarter dead and three quarters alive. And if I was not happy with three quarters? Then I would keep hunting. What else is life for?

He says, life is for making the best of and right now is the best it has been. He wishes and she wishes she felt as he does.

She murdered her baby. She did not want her dead but couldn't keep her alive and people say that death by drowning is the sweetest. For her daughter she chose the best death of all.

Men and women lie on striped beach towels or ones with palm trees, dolphins or yellow ball suns. They rub oil on brown and red bodies. Lie back in the sticky scent of coconut and watermelon, swat flies, fidget, turn on their stomachs, backs, sides. Pick up paperback books, read four lines, read those four lines again, scratch, fidget, sit up, lie down.

Fancy a swim?

Not yet. All right. Wait for me.

Men and women pick their clumsy way over hot sand and pebbles. Stand at the edge of the sea with the sun in their eyes and arms dangling. Strips of puce-coloured skin show at the edges of their bathing suits.

They wade into the sea, splash about. Call, this is the life. Feel chilled, return to their towels. Start all over again.

Today he is building her a sand castle with turrets and towers and ice lolly stick flags. There are conch shells around the windows and a moat the size of his arm.

He has enlisted the help of a twelve-year-old in emerald green swimming trunks. The boy is chief shell-collector and moat-digger. The more troublesome tasks, such as wall-building, he is resolved to accomplish alone.

He says, your palace awaits. He pulls her to her feet. See, the doors and windows are open. Walk with me, he says, on carpets as deep as seas. Look at the marble-topped tables and Italian glass, the stone fireplaces, the coloured rugs, the sunken bookcases, the lacquer cabinets, the gilt looking glasses.

Behind them, the boy holds out the hem of her thin summer dress like a train.

Lie with me, he says, in chairs the size of beds, in beds the size of rooms, in rooms it will take us whole days to walk through.

He says, if I died now I could die happy.

She says, I haven't lived happy yet.

He leaves her alone for the afternoon. She lies hot and still. Sweat stings her eyes and snakes over her cheeks into her mouth.

He returns with apples, chocolate, thin sharp wine, a spray of hibiscus and a packet of painkillers.

The next day they climb a small mountain, following a path picked out in painted rocks, pink, blue and garden-gate green. A family of white goats climbs with them for a while, walking in single file.

He takes photographs: views, goats, her, rocks, her, flowering grasses. They drink bottled water, warm. Eke out the chocolate squares for four miles and then devour the rest in one sitting. The air is filled with birds in discordant chorus. The same snatches over and over.

At the top, they write their names in lines of stones. At the bottom, he buys a loaf of bread and another packet of painkillers. Four days, four packets.

In the evenings, in the rented room with thick wall hangings and their collection of sea treasures, he empties his pills onto the table and counts them into piles of ten. He has more than a hundred. More than enough.

He laughs a lot. Says, the only way to feel alive is to choose life.

Each night he scoops the pills back into the jars, twists the child-safe lids and puts them in the bathroom cabinet next to the shaving foam, toothpaste and condoms. He says he is choosing life. It makes him feel like a king.

Over milky coffee and cinnamon cakes in a bar with wall-to-wall paintings of men's faces, he pours three heaped spoons of sugar into his mouth and can barely close it. Granules spew out the sides and fall onto his Hawaiian shirt. It is too bold, too bright, too flowery for this small curtained bar in an unmarked street.

He says, those who are afraid to die are the same people who are afraid to live. Or love, he says. Or laugh.

The bar is too quiet or he is too loud and she thinks, he means me.

Her baby was so small she held her under the water with one hand. She felt her rock under her fingers. She stayed until the water turned cold. Then, together, they dripped over the mat.

She thinks, to kill the pain it may be necessary to kill

myself. We may opt for a breathless, dreamless sleep, but our reasons could not be more different.

In the middle of the night she wakes and everything is purple – window, walls, carpet, wardrobe, dressing table. Her baby is here too. Clamped to her left breast. There is sleep around the baby's eyes and Magda wipes it away with the ball of her little finger.

The baby bites her breast. The skin on her belly is stretched taut like a drum and she keeps drinking and drinking. Her hair is like cotton wool. She wants to sleep but doesn't want to stop drinking.

Magda tries to push a finger between the baby's gums and her nipple but there is no room and her daughter will not make room. She's hurting her with her teeth. Magda tries to pull her breast away but her baby is stronger than her. She is drinking her life.

Magda wants to crack her daughter's head like a coconut. She wants to be a good mother. She wants to help her sleep peacefully. She wants the best for her daughter.

When she was a girl Magda had a friend who was everything she ever wanted. She was so much more than anything she'd had. She said Magda helped her to live. Certainly Magda helped her not to die. She remembers hoisting her friend out of a steaming pink bath. Afternoons sitting in ambulances, her pale arms leaking sticky red onto the white tin floor.

Magda did not know how anyone could hurt so much because she believed that everything was manageable. She told her friend, all you have to do is keep thinking of the good things. She couldn't imagine a time when the good things would not be enough.

For a long time Magda was her friend's good thing. Then it changed. Now he is her good thing. But good things are like ice lollies left in the sun.

In the bathroom cabinet the purple painkillers stand in lines like an army awaiting orders. Left right, death life, left right.

Outside on the beach, a stray dog barks. Matchstick ribs in hairless beige. Flies on his legs. Eyes like cracked plates. He smells sweet and rancid, trapped in a body too strong for his own good.

The purple pills sit in Magda's hand. Little eggs of potential.

During the night, they argue. Her arms crossed over her chest, Magda starts to moan and sob, then she cannot stop. The yellow light from the moon illuminates him, stretched out on the rented bed, the sheet falling around him.

They lie on the bed as the sun rises. They have made a

choice. He wants to hold on to the good before it turns bad. She wants an end to aimlessness. They smoke their way through a packet of cigarettes.

She has a pain in her stomach. She is sweating. She sees the purple room and the purple furniture, his jeans and trainers in a pile on the floor. A warm wind stirs the curtains.

She smokes slowly, inhales deeply. When she moves her body to make a pot of coffee, her legs tremble. She slumps on the edge of the bed, finding it hard to breathe.

She says, the dead are all around me, the dead outnumber the living, the living are not always alive.

They drain two bottles of wine. She curls up on the bed, coiling deep into herself. Cries into the sheet, then untangles herself and goes to sit with him at the table.

He is counting the pills into two piles. He wraps his arm around her, and they talk in low voices.

Do you love me? You do? You do?

Then they are silent. They kiss, walk back to the bed and swallow the purple pills with warm white wine. He sings softly as they lie on the bed, listening to the sea. They do not turn from each other. The air carries soft and spiked smells.

The stars are gone. It is nearly the next day. She is alive and he is dead. Dead because he swallowed a hundred pills.

Alive because she swallowed twenty-five, slipping the rest from hand to pocket.

She lies next to her pale brown man. She cries because he found and rescued her when it was impossible, because he died with clarity and choice. He is still here, with her daughter. Her two loves feeding on air.

5. Cinnamon and pomegranate seeds

Her head aches. Her eyes ache. In her ears the sound of the sea smashing against rocks. She is a woman in black. A woman who cannot cry. A woman holding on to the hand of a Greek child who says: drink this, light that, kneel, stand, speak.

White church on a cliff. Smells of incense and old flowers. A priest with a long beard offers up prayers for a dead man he never met. A man from a different land. A man who would not understand his words or his meaning.

We have eternal life, says the priest, and it has a beginning, a middle, an end and a new beginning.

He would laugh. Now, he would say. Now is all we have.

Outside, light blinds the people in black. They squint, blink, stretch, look up. Yellow ball sun. Sky as blue as a crayoned picture.

The landlady's house is packed full of statues and ornaments: china women, children, fruit bowls and flowers. They eat okra and dogfish; sweets made of cinnamon and pomegranate seeds. The landlady's daughter, Somah, makes coffee, puts a cup in Magda's hand.

Man gone now, she says. What will you do?

Do?

Magda is holding on so tight to her coffee cup that it is a part of her body. Mouth empty. Tongue a heavy, swollen thing.

In Magda's room, shadows flick against the walls. She smokes in the dark, knees drawn up to her chest under the thin sheet.

There are thoughts like knives: he is a pale brown body in a puddle of urine. A fist squeezing her heart like a small dry lemon.

And there are thoughts like spoons: she remembers him as an echo, the last drop of water in a bowl in the sun, something golden but gone.

I should miss him, she thinks. But I do not. I am untouched. Untouchable. He said: I love you like a fire and I did not want to burn.

Tears, when they come, are dry before they hit the ground. Leave a snake trail of salt.

Foreign country dreams of friends and strangers, forgetting which is which. She wakes in sheets wound round and round and still it is not morning. Washed-out light. The sound of water splashing against stones.

6. Stories with wings

Greek town built around an alabaster statue of a man who is half fish. Boys roll stones in the dust around his tail. As Magda walks towards them, they stand, pulling their shorts to their waists. Immediately they slip down to their hips, their thin bodies slippery as waxed floors.

Magda walks between stalls laden with olives, peaches, bananas, melons, grapes. Sticky sweets the size of footballs, flowers and bread. The air is hot. She buys a bottle of mineral water and after drinking, presses its cool ribbed plastic against her forehead.

There is a bar with glass-topped tables. Magda sits at a man's table. She does not know the person she has become. Same two hands, two eyes, two feet. But the invisible things are not, cannot be as they were. He has green eyes. Green with splashes of brown.

She tells him: I used to be a woman who cared about things: children with empty bellies and arms like pipe-cleaners, the poisoned sea, the hole in the sky. I used to write letters, drink wine, spin round and round until I could no longer stand up. I used to be that woman. I used to do those things.

The man is silent. He remains silent for a long time, big fingers circling the rim of a white china cup. Then he says: I used to be a storyteller. I earned my living by the edge of my tongue and the colours in front of my eyes. But I dried up in a village where the people wanted words like eagles and I had only the feathers of a sparrow. I told them: my wife is dying. They said: go home, come back when you can tell us something that is different from the lives we know. Everywhere wives are dying. We want stories with wings.

Stories with wings. Magda is silent. She is thinking: what use are stories with wings? She says: what use are stories with wings?

The storyteller smiles and this time it is with the whole of himself.

Stories change lives, he says. That is their purpose.

This night, the night that follows her meeting with the

storyteller, the night when she is thinking that stories may change lives and, if so, she has stories and stories and stories, Magda has a visitor. The Greek girl with eyes that are too big for her face. They drink coffee, eat baklava, listen to the whisper of the waves.

Magda asks: would you like a story?

And when Somah says: yes, curling her long legs underneath her, Magda says: all right, I'll start at the beginning.

But where is that? She pauses, looks around the cluttered room. Says: Magda's mother died the day Magda was born. Says: that is one beginning.

Uneasy silence spreading, filling the room.

Father, she says. That's another beginning.

Looking for words, sentences, sounds to make shapes in the air.

Here's another beginning, says Magda. A significant one. And an ending. Magda met her second mother in a supermarket. For several weeks she had been going there to look at the women in rain coats and patent shoes, their brown and black stockinged legs patchy with mud and fluff.

She followed them as they navigated their trolleys around the aisles. She enjoyed watching them make their selections; squeezing peaches, avocadoes, tomatoes and melons, lining up packets of rice, knots and twists of spaghetti and bags of bright yellow beans.

When the supermarket closed, she sat on the strip of green behind the car park and ate chocolate washed down with fizzy orange. She kept lists in the back of an exercise book in her satchel. Short lists.

Magda was tempted by a woman who filled her trolley with flour, butter and glacé cherries. She imagined the smells in her house, sweet heat rising from the oven, a kitchen table groaning under scones and buns.

But the cake-maker often had a little boy with her, a red-faced, long-fingered little boy who put candles, bin liners and baked beans into her trolley whenever her back was turned. Magda did not want to share her mother with a brother.

Magda says: there was a red-haired woman whose lips were purple, eyes ringed with rainbow shadows. High heels made her teeter and lean forward. Her fingernails clacked along the shelves. As well as crisps, frozen pizzas, plastic cartons of olives and cheeses that oozed, the red-haired woman put long bottles of rum into her basket.

One afternoon when rain was spattering the windows of the supermarket and Magda was bored with making shapes out of clusters of drops, she saw the red-haired woman at the check-out. She paid by cheque, using a slim gold pen to sign her name.

She was heading for the door. Magda followed her. Out

to her car. Shiny metallic blue with a hole in the roof to let the wind whistle through. The rain in the air made everything damp and luminous.

Magda asked: can I come home with you?

She was a scrap in a duffle coat with sleeves that ended above her elbows. Her woollen tights were filled with holes and her shoes held together with mud.

The woman with red hair and rainbow eyes said: haven't you got a home of your own?

No, Magda said.

And how do you know you'll like mine?

Magda smiled a lot, standing there in the rain and scuffing her toes in the gravel and the woman must have liked what she saw because she opened the passenger door with the sweetest of clicks and said: get in.

Magda says: it was warm inside her car. The windscreen wipers made everything blurred then clear, blurred then clear: trees, people standing at bus stops, small houses with big lawns and rows of flowers like cups.

The woman said: you can stay one night and then you will have to go.

Yes, said Magda. One night, she said.

There was a spare bedroom with a single bed swamped with blankets. A small square of window looked out over red-tiled roofs and chimneys. Pigeons strutted and preened. The last of the rain dripped and hissed.

It's lovely, Magda said.

One night, the woman said.

She made Magda sit in her cream-coloured bath and scrub her body, behind her ears, under her nails. Then, because Magda had no clothes other than the ones they peeled off her, she dressed Magda in a jumper that reached her knees and socks like flippers around her feet.

The woman said: you look almost decent.

Magda said: I am.

The woman fed Magda tomato soup and toast with jam.

She said: that's what children like isn't it?

Yes, Magda said.

She opened a box of chocolates and let Magda eat the ones with soft centres. She drank rum, watching the ice cubes bob and clink in her glass. Magda sipped the firewater, said she had tasted it before.

The woman said: you are a peculiar girl.

Yes, Magda said.

Where do you come from?

Far away.

How did you get here?

I ran.

Why did you run?

Because I was unhappy.

You can stay one night, she said.

Yes, Magda said. She said: thank you.

Magda does not know the person she has become. Now she is a woman who talks, who talks and talks. Who paces around the rented room, touching books, trailing fingers over window glass, and all the time she is talking.

Magda says: Magda dreamed she set sail on a cotton wool sea in a boat of feathers held together with string. The distant shore was made of marshmallows and she was geting closer all the time.

Girl overboard.

The cry rang throughout the boat and Magda was swimming for that island as hard as she could. Faster than the boat or the fish or the birds.

The next morning Magda had tea in a china cup the size of her face. Brittle cereal swimming in condensed milk. Her flippered feet swung like pendulums under the kitchen table.

The red-haired woman said: I have to go to work.

Yes, Magda said.

And you have to leave.

Yes, Magda said.

She gave Magda ten pounds. She said: take care of yourself. And: don't steal or hurt people.

She handed Magda an apple to put in her pocket, then a packet of digestive biscuits, then a peanut butter sandwich. She was looking around the kitchen to see what else she could give her when Magda started to cry. Her tears splashed the front of her dress and the chess board linoleum.

The woman said: don't do that. She said: I don't want a daughter.

Magda watched her drive away in her shiny metallic blue car that the wind whistled through, then she sat on the front step and ate her digestive biscuits.

Magda was still sitting there when the woman got home from work.

Magda said: you look pretty.

The woman said: you can't come in.

Magda sat listening to the sounds of the house: African drums on the stereo, banging doors, the whirr and clunk of the hot water system. Magda's legs felt cold and knotted. She decided to walk around the block and then come back.

Magda was seventeen houses away when she saw the woman running towards her. Her coat was undone and her red hair flopped across her face in soapy ribbons.

All right, she said. You win, she said.

The woman's breath was loud in the street. Under an olive-coloured blouse, her breasts heaved.

7. In the see-through house

Somah's mother calls for her to go home but later, after she has eaten her meal and cleaned her teeth and climbed into sleep-clothes that have pictures of dragons on them, she sneaks out of the house. Back in the beach hut, wrapped up in Magda's sleeping bag, she says: more.

And there is more. So Magda says: Magda's mother had many lovers. They came with flowers for her and chocolates for Magda. They ruffled Magda's hair, made her sit on their laps and call them uncle.

Magda muddled their names. Watched Greg redden as she called him Guy, heard Guy stammer as she called him Rob. Magda's mother laughed. She was beginning to like Magda.

Greg wanted to take them on holiday. He wanted to wear Hawaiian shirts, he said, and drink blue drinks with paper umbrellas. He bought tickets, arranged passports, filled a suitcase with shorts.

The day they left, Greg fell down a flight of stairs, his suitcase spilling a posy of purples, yellows and pinks on to the street. Greg went to hospital. Magda and her mother went on holiday.

Magda's mother fell out the sides of her bikini. Lobster-pink on a sun-lounger. She waved her glass at Magda, beads of sweat dripping off the end of her nose.

Do you think I'm going brown?

Marco was an old man. His hands were like bits of tree. He took them to restaurants where people spoke in whispers.

Marco said he wanted to marry Magda's mother. Magda's mother said she wanted to marry Marco. They married on the sand in bathing suits. His belly stuck out in front like a beach ball.

Marco said: I love you.

Magda's mother said: I love you.

Magda said: what about me?

They said: the three of us will be very happy.

But Magda never planned on sharing her mother.

In Marco's house made of windows, Magda looked out at the sea or walked around his rooms, smashing his cups and plates.

Marco said: it doesn't matter.

Magda stopped.

Magda's mother and Marco were always in the bedroom and when they weren't, they were piling trays with prawns and newspapers to take back in there with them.

Are you terribly bored?

Yes, Magda said, terribly.

Magda's mother said: I've discovered love so late.

Magda said: it's much too soon for me.

Magda dreamed Marco was lying on his back in the middle of a long table and she and her mother were eating him. She dreamed half of him was in the road under a truck, and the rest was curled around a tree. She dreamed he was on fire and her mother was trying to blow him out.

Magda's mother said: Marco is a good man.

Yes, Magda said.

Kind and gentle.

Yes.

And a marvellous lover.

Magda said: I don't want to know. But she did.

Her mother said: he licks me all over like I'm ice cream.

Magda said: that's disgusting.

Magda says: Marco had a servant. They called him the

hired help. He was seventeen years old with pitted skin and black hair tied back with a shoelace. Magda asked him to lick her all over like she was ice cream, but he was frightened he would lose his job.

They were in the kitchen. He was chopping coriander. It smelled of perfume.

Magda said: I won't tell anyone.

She lay on the kitchen floor and lifted her dress. There were windows in the ceiling. Through them the sky was very white. His mouth felt like a mouse.

Magda giggled.

His breath was harsh and strange in the big room.

Magda said: stop it.

He said: I can't.

Magda said: tell me you love me.

He said: I love you.

Magda closed her eyes and tried to imagine what it must be like to be her mother, enjoying this.

Magda says: her mother sat on the bed in her room and looked past her at the sky.

Marco has a weak heart, she said. He needs rest.

Yes, Magda said.

I might lose him.

Yes, Magda said.

It would be the end of everything.

The house was full of whispers. The hired help tried to grab Magda in the hall. Her mother crept into her room at night. Marco's words were thin as air. The wind tried to blow them into the sea.

Then one morning Magda woke and the sea was perfectly smooth.

Her mother said: Marco is dead.

They sat in their big see-through house and looked out. Sitting so still they could feel the house rock. So much sea. Everything was blue and moving.

Magda heard the creaking of the chandelier. Felt her bottom in the chair, the chair on the floor, the floor on the rocks, the rocks on the seabed. Pinhead small and yet so large she could have swallowed the sea.

There were patches of light in the sky.

Magda's mother said: Marco made me laugh more than any man I have known.

They walked around the house, lay full-length on the carpets.

Mine, her mother said.

They opened all the windows until the sound of the sea filled every corner.

We are rich, she said.

For a while after Marco's death, he lived with them. In the big see-through house by the sea. They laid a place for him at the table, filled his plate, included him in conversations. Walking by the sea, Marco pointed out rocks or shells or coils of sea worms. Magda's mother's heels left holes in the sand like dot-to-dot puzzles.

Magda says: Magda's problem: how to tell her mother that she loved her. She watched her move around the kitchen, her hair was piled on top of her head, her bare feet made sucking noises on the tiles.

Magda said: I'm glad.

Glad?

Her mother cracked an egg on the side of a glass bowl. Turned the shell upside down and scooped out the last traces of yolk with her finger.

Glad, Magda said, moving around on her chair like it was hot. That you're here and so am I.

Her mother was looking at the book on the counter in front of her and her hands were on her hips.

Really glad, Magda said.

Magda heard the second hand creak around the clock's enormous face.

Really, really glad.

Magda, her mother said. And she turned to face her. There was flour in her red hair and spotting the front of her jumper. What are you trying to tell me?

That I'm glad we're here together, Magda said.

Yes, her mother said. But I wish Marco was here too.

Magda says: Magda's mother was in the bath cutting her nails. Chipped red crescents collected on the mat. She was all beige above the suds. Beige and freckled.

Magda said: it's nice. Being here. With you.

Yes.

I like you, Magda said.

I like you too.

It was not what Magda wanted to hear. She said: I really like you.

Magda's mother stopped soaping her shoulders and looked at Magda, hard, as if she was a tricky crossword clue.

I know Magda, she said.

8. Peeled fruit

Rented room. This is what Magda sees: one bed (bedspread coming away in loose handfuls), one small table, two chairs, beauty products displayed like white and gold trinkets, strangers' names scratched into paint. This is what Magda hears: the snarl of a sea that wants to smash and smash and smash.

It is a white room with blue-flowered curtains across the window. Today Somah has not come, so it is an empty room. Just Magda, the walls and the furniture. But the furniture keeps moving and the walls swell and shrink back from Magda so that no matter how she stretches and twists her body, she cannot touch anything solid.

This is what Magda thinks: I can go back. There is a place to go back to.

And this is what Magda thinks: I cannot go back. There is nowhere to go back to.

Late afternoon. A man stands in the doorway to Magda's room. Dark hair sweeps across his pear-shaped head.

I am Somah's uncle Marius, he bows slightly. I want to welcome you.

Thank you.

May I come in?

He is inside her room and his eyes are like hands.

You have lovely things.

Yes.

Somah likes you.

Yes.

May I sit down?

He is on her bed, spreading his legs wide, patting a space on the rumpled white sheet. Folding herself in to it, Magda can hear his breath, the ticking of his watch. She sees the shiny hardness of his arms.

I've seen you walking in the market, he says. The way you move, the way you look. You're lonely.

Lonely?

You need comfort.

Comfort?

You need protection.

I can look after myself.

Your man is gone.

Yes, she says. No.

In your country, he says, you have free sex?

Free sex?

He laughs, tracing the curve of black hairs that sit on his lip.

You English girls like it.

His hand is on her hand. He smells of Old Spice and garlic.

I know all about you, he says.

She says: I don't want this. But her voice is quiet and small.

I don't want this. She tries to make her voice louder.

I know who you are, he says. I know what you want.

The heat of his body. The pressure of his ringed fingers.

You want this.

Do I?

You know that you do.

His hands in her hair pull so that small sharp tears blur her eyes. He is breathing too much of her air. She pushes him back and he falls on to the threadbare rug and bangs his head on the floor.

For a moment, everything is still. Like the pause before applause or the thundering of rain.

Bitch, he says, standing and smoothing his clothes. Women are all cock-teasing whores.

He spits a clear jet of saliva which lands on her cheek, slips on to her neck and crawls towards her breast.

Magda thinks: a layer of skin is missing. I am peeled fruit; my centre smells so sweet I am a walking invitation: eat me.

Outside, wind flattens tops of thin trees. A door bangs and bangs. Magda sees a goat in a doorway shrink in fear. People hide in corners, waiting for the wind to pass through empty streets.

Arms outstretched, Somah is running around the fishman, tomato-red skirt clinging to her body and trailing behind. Glitter of beads at her throat.

Stormdancing, as if the wind was rain and she could take it inside her.

Magda walking down the stairs, feels like a child at a party wanting to join in a game.

Somah's sweaty, gritty hand.

The wind beats on their shoulders and hair. Flying dust blasts their faces. A ball of straw rushes up the track towards them, they do not move and it grazes their shins.

At night the wind slinks away, leaving clean streets. Dust settles elsewhere. Buildings, like pencil drawings, have sharp outlines. People move lighter, slice the air with pointed strides.

Magda thinks: the calm after the storm is a radiant one. It can hurt your eyes.

9. Stone baby

This night, because the light is fading and stars are prick-
ing the sky like needles, Magda tells Somah: I have a
child.

Somah is all bracelets and eyes. Dark hair slips out of
an elastic band.

A child?

Yes, a girl.

She is with you?

Yes.

Can I see her?

Beads of sweat string across Somah's forehead and rest
in the hollow above her Vaselined lips.

This is my treasure.

She flashes a thin silver bangle at Magda.

Now you.

Treasure one: a photograph of Missing, lying across Magda's belly like a fish.

Somah holds the picture so close to her face that it touches her nose.

Your baby?

Yes.

Where is she?

Here.

In this room?

Yes.

I can't see her.

Look, says Magda.

Somah peers under the bed, in the rucksack, behind the books, under piles of clothes.

She's not here.

Yes she is. Close your eyes.

Magda puts her stone in Somah's hand. Smooth and grey.

My baby is in here.

In Somah's other hand, Magda places a china cup.

She is in here too.

Somah opens her eyes.

Magda says: my baby is in everything. I see her all the time. I hear her too.

She is a dead baby.

Yes, says Magda. No.

She is a stone baby, says Somah. I will call her the stone baby.

Somah brings flowers for the stone baby. Jasmine flowers threaded on a string. They fill the room with their perfume. She winds them around the grey stone, sets them on the window in the light.

10. What to do with a friend

Magda tells Somah: once there was a yellow-haired boy playing with crabs on the rocks. He didn't want to be Magda's friend and she didn't know what to do with a friend. And still they found themselves talking, holding the hard backs of sea creatures that kicked the air.

It was late afternoon. The air blew under their clothes and prickled their skin. His shoelaces were undone, trailing in the rock pools as she walked behind him.

Here's a crab, Magda said, holding one out to him. Pink and purple. Almost a handful.

I can find my own. Dom looked round long enough to

61

see that she was not of much interest to him. But he liked the crab. Magda could see that. The way his eyes sat on it. He was stroking the crab with his eyes.

And still he said: it's not a very good crab.

Yes, it is.

No it's not. Look. He stopped. Turned to face Magda. It has a leg missing.

So?

So it's not perfect.

But he couldn't take his eyes off it. Stretching out a finger, touching its flat underbelly.

Dom said: crabs like that are easy. To find a really good crab, you have to look hard and know what you're looking for. You have to wait a lot and get wet.

He kicked a rock. There was a small hole in the toe of his shoe. Magda could see his red sock.

You don't know what you're doing, he said.

He said: go away.

Magda pushed him on the shoulder. His shirt was damp and gritty with sand. He pushed her back. Hard. She stumbled. There above the sea with the white foam splashing up to get them.

Magda dropped her crab. She heard its shell crack. Its legs were like greedy fingers then. Pushing and pulling. The boy picked the crab up and put it in his pocket. Magda walked back to the house.

Magda says: Magda went out that night when the moon was pale behind a cloud and the stars were like torches on low power. So much wriggling on the rocks. Water pools jumped. Tiny shells crawled. In the dark her shoes crunched and slid.

The crabs were puny. White-shelled and busy. Magda put a few in a bucket and watched them crawl over each other and up the blue plastic walls.

That night Magda dreamed she was a huge crab in a cave under the sea and the yellow-haired boy wanted her so badly he wept.

You are the most perfect crab, he said.

Come home with me, he said.

I'll give you everything you want, he said.

Magda woke and he was looking in her window.

Magda said: I was dreaming about you.

He said: what did you dream?

You had found your perfect crab.

He said: come quickly.

When Magda stumbled he grabbed her hand.

Quickly, he said. Run, he said.

So they ran and there was no where are we going, just shifting stones under their feet and salt on their faces. Magda liked the criss-cross scratches at the tops of his arms. The dank wood smell of his hair as they sat in a hole in the rocks.

The clouds changed patterns in the sky. Dom stood close to the edge of the rocks, toes curled over, arms stretched wide.

There's nothing to stop me jumping, he said.

In a minute I could be dead, he said. Try it.

He held out his hand but Magda stepped back.

I don't want to.

Why not?

I might fall.

You won't fall, he said. I'll keep hold of your hand.

He reached for her again. Come on.

Magda felt the blood in her face, the wind pressing her nightshirt against her legs.

Come on.

Magda says: Magda stood at the edge of the cliff, holding Dom's hand. The sea swirled and spat. Dark in the heart. She was squeezing his fingers between her fingers and looking down.

Do you like it?

Dom's voice was carried on the wind.

Yes.

Are you still frightened?

Yes.

You're frightened and you like it?

Yes, she said. Yes.

11. Happiness barometer

Another day, Magda tells Somah: when Magda and her mother walked around the town, people looked. Magda's mother was a widow in fuchsia lipstick. She bought arms full of flowers but instead of laying them on her husband's grave, she arranged them in wine bottles on the windowsills in the house.

She bought expensive wines, frozen gateaux, black grapes, raspberries and mangoes. She purchased dresses with no straps and shoes that wound around her ankles. She lived in the see-through house as if it was filled with guests.

But no one came. Not even the dead man's sister.

So Magda's mother said: hello. And: hello, again, until the woman standing in front of her in the post office queue had to turn and smile her thinnest smile.

Hello.

Marco's sister Envicta had white hair scraped into a ponytail. She wore a dark coat. Her lips were lavender.

Magda's mother said: I'm happy to see you.

Envicta spoke so quietly, swallowing up her words, Magda's mother had to move closer to hear her.

Magda says: Envicta arrived at Magda's mother's house in a brown wool dress. She had smeared her eyes with olive-coloured cream.

She said: I can't stay long.

She perched on the edge of Marco's cream-coloured sofa, sipped slowly at the long drink Magda's mother made her.

Envicta said: the house feels different.

Magda's mother said: the rooms were filled with Marco even after he died. We had to chase him out – she laughed. But he comes back.

Envicta said: you're lucky. I can't see him at all.

Envicta said: I close my eyes but all I get is the shape of his head. No features, she said, nothing that is Marco at all.

Magda's mother said: his eyes were shaped like almonds.

She said: they were fat in the middle and filled with light.

She said: his left eye was smaller than his right.

Envicta cried then. Small tears, barely water at all, except she was wiping them away with the corner of her sleeve.

His eyes were flecked with yellow, Envicta said.

Yes, said Magda's mother.

They ate in silence. Sitting at the long table under the chandelier. The soup was hot. They blew on their spoons and still their mouths burned. Envicta refused the gateau but Magda's mother cut her a slice anyway and she ate it anyway, leaving only crumbs.

Magda says: there were more dinners. Envicta stayed later and later.

When her husband rang, Envicta said: you don't own me.

Magda's mother put her arm around Envicta as she cried. Magda's mother with her arm around Marco's sister, the white-haired woman like a collapsing chair.

Envicta said: I live half a life.

Envicta said: all the time a part of me sleeps.

Magda's mother said: it doesn't have to be that way.

And Envicta cried more. Her face in her hands.

Envicta said: you don't understand.

Envicta said: you can't understand.

Then one night as she stood at the door and didn't want to go but said she couldn't stay, Envicta said: only you understand.

Half-way down the stairs, Magda felt it. Something hard-edged that stuck a bruise in her ribs.

Magda's mother said: stay.

Envicta said: I can't.

Magda's mother said: you can, you can, you can. And each time she said it, Magda saw Envicta shudder.

Envicta said: I am a wife.

Envicta said: I am a mother.

Envicta said: I have built a life and I can't imagine another.

Magda says: Envicta stood on the steps in the warm rain. There was mud on her stockings and the hem of her coat.

She said: I can't stay long. But I can't stay away. I never used to cry or laugh but now I do both extravagantly.

Magda says: Envicta was barefoot on the rocks when her husband Enario came to see her. He crept up behind her. He enjoyed watching her jump.

He wanted Envicta like so. And she wanted to be like so. So she tried again, walking on the rocks, thinking before she spoke, speaking before she knew what was in her heart.

They walked. And he talked. And they slipped again in the same holes.

That night, Magda saw her mother hold another woman's feet in her lap. The room was quiet. Short candles sputtered on the windowsill. There were no words. Just the ragged sound of breath and the sh-sh of the sea.

Magda stood in the doorway. She saw them. She had the feeling of being far out and lost. Nothing to hold on to but the sleeve of her jumper. She lowered her eyes, looked at her own feet until she saw clearly their whiteness on the carpet.

When Magda looked again, the two women's heads were very close and the quietness outside was between them like a crystal. Like something hard and pure.

Magda could have stayed on the edge of something about to happen. She could have gone to bed, curled under her duvet and listened to the wind on the sea. Envicta looked up to see Magda standing in the doorway, her jumper bunched in her fists: then they were fighting on the carpet.

Magda scratched Envicta's eyes. She bit the flesh at the back of her arm. She felt her bones underneath her fingers like old twigs she could snap. Envicta beat her off, one hand in front of her face, the other flailing in the air.

Envicta said: you're mad.

Her breath caught inside her chest. And Magda was laughing because she didn't feel mad. Not mad at all. A bird was trapped inside her body and beating and flapping its enormous wings.

Envicta was covered with small cuts. There were handfuls of her white hair on the carpet. Her lips were very pale.

She said: don't touch me, as Magda's mother tried to help her back on to the sofa.

Envicta said: you should have stopped her. She did not look at Magda or her mother as she walked out of the room.

Magda says: in the see-through house, Magda and Envicta took it in turns to win Magda's mother. Magda grabbed, was brash. Envicta murmured and minced. Magda came from the front. Envicta crept in from the side. Envicta called Magda wild. Magda called her zero.

And still Magda watched them through the windows, their arms around each other's waists. And the whispers. Magda threw stones into the sea, kicked boulders off the cliffs, her full weight behind them. The splash sending a broken fountain into the air.

We are always searching for a love, Magda's mother said. Whatever else we call it.

Magda didn't know if she agreed. She had seen her mother happy with a love and unhappy with it. Magda wondered whether happiness was the right barometer with which to measure your life. And, if not, what else was there?

12. A story about shrinking

Sun beats down. Waves crawl in, dribble out, smooth shells, stir up stones. And here she is again with the Greek girl and she is talking. Talking and talking. I'll tell you a story, Magda says, about shrinking.

Envicta's husband Enario came to dinner. They all dressed up. Magda's mother in white. Envicta in pink. Magda in a shade of navy blue. They sat at the table under the chandelier and sliced their beans so they fitted neatly into their mouths.

It was as if there was a fire in the centre of the room, burning a hole in the carpet, licking up the tablecloth, roasting their toes. And none of them could take their eyes off it. And none of them could speak of it.

Enario smelled of cigarettes but his breath was sweet. He sat too close. Talked too loud. Was big and out of place in the see-through house. He stretched in his chair and his belly rested against the table. Pale checked shirt. Sharp creases.

He tapped the table gently but still the cutlery jumped. He would not look at Envicta and she would not look at him, but the fire was in their laps.

Enario said: you can't grab at new things without making sacrifices.

Envicta jumped up from the table and stood there shaking, her arms twitching at her sides.

You don't know, she said. And you don't want me to know.

She ran from the room. Stood under a moon that made her feel she was shrinking, breath by breath, being swallowed into the stars.

Magda says: Envicta crouched in a corner of the bathroom. Folded up inside her dressing gown so that only her hair was visible. White on white tiles.

When Enario came home from work, she said, I used to race to meet him because he gave me an outline. He coloured me in. You're home, I'd say. What can I get you? I'd say. A drink. And then? And then?

I had everything. A neat-fitting life. Smooth walls, visible ceilings, a way of being in the world that made me inside of it, not out. But I saw how happy Marco was with you, she said, and I wanted that for myself. I swapped my old life for a new one with you. But I cannot be a new person.

No.

I am the same woman.

Yes.

And I don't like her any more now than I did then.

Magda says: Envicta packed her dresses and books, her collection of blown glass figures and the array of stockings and bottles that were strewn across the bathroom.

Enario came to fetch her in his big scarlet car with a small hole in the roof; he had opened it half-way. He loaded her bags into the boot, jiggled the change in his pocket.

Envicta's hands were wriggling together and pulling apart.

Enario said: come now.

She said: I can't, and she said: you don't understand. Please, she said. Please. I want to say goodbye.

Enario climbed into the car and started the engine. Leaned over and opened the passenger door.

Get in, he said.

Looking back and over her shoulder, moving so slowly she was barely moving at all, Envicta climbed into Enario's car.

I am doing the right thing, she said. It's better this way.

Magda says: Magda's mother was out on the rocks. Magda was showing her the inside of a shell that was purple and so smooth her fingers could not help touching it.

Lovely, she said. Lovely.

Magda's mother heard the slam of the car door and the crunch of gravel as Envicta and Enario pulled away. She looked out to where the sea and sky met and stroked the perfect thing in her hands.

Magda says: Magda's mother prowled around the house. She could not lie still.

She said: the twisting sheets feel like ropes.

So she walked. In and out of the rooms she owned. Looked out of the windows.

Said: all I see is Envicta.

They went for a drive through the blue-black night. Magda and her mother. Sagging vines in the headlights. Misty mountains poked the sky.

Magda's mother twitched in the car seat, played music that scratched the inside of Magda's head.

Where are we going?

We're not going anywhere.

Foot down hard on the accelerator.

Magda's mother said: the thing is to keep moving.
Swinging in to more blue-blackness.

Black roads like tar, twisting, turning and doubling back. Ended up circling Envicta's house. Walled garden full of flowering trees and statues; the walls washed salmon pink.

Magda says: Envicta sent a letter. Tiny squashed together words on thick paper. Magda's mother read them aloud as Magda followed her into a room crowded with canvases. Hand prints. Body prints. Layers of yellow and orange and green.

Of all the things I regret, Envicta said, this stands out: I glimpsed the top of the mountain, but the bottom appealed to me more.

Magda's mother burned Envicta's letter, holding it over the ring of the cooker, watching it blacken and flare orange. Fragments flew around the kitchen like dying insects, settled on teacups and on the corners of shelves.

Magda says: Magda saw Envicta one more time. She had shrunk again, her body pulled in as if she was wrapped around with rope. She turned white when she saw Magda, so white her hair looked blue.

How is your mother?
Well.

Well? Tell her you saw me.

Yes.

And tell her there are no more surprises in my life. One day I will eat fresh asparagus or mangoes for dinner. Another I will wear a new pair of snake-skin shoes. Another I will walk through all the rooms in my house and wonder who will come after me.

After Envicta had gone, Magda stood in a shop doorway, pushing her fists hard against the frame. Thirty seconds, twenty-nine, twenty-eight. Magda's whole body was a knot, squeezed tight and when she ran into the middle of the street, her arms floated up and out from the sides of her body as if they were wings. Again Magda did it. Again and again. For the feel of it. The magical unstoppable feel of her arms lighter than air.

13. Falling

Sitting on the edge of the bed, Magda thinks: the hut is moving. I am sliding into the sea. Everything is slipping and there is no way to stop it.

She runs her fingers over the sticky wood of the bed-head, digs out a thick, soft splinter. Hears her breath; slow, deep, in and out.

A light touch on her hair. The almost imperceptible pressure of a hand in hers. Chill like a second body around her body. Then Missing is gone and Magda feels herself shrinking. Small again. Grubby and hot.

Magda curls and uncurls her hands. The air hurts. So does clenching her teeth and crying. But she cannot stop. She puts on dirty clothes. Comforted by hiding her body and inhaling her own smell.

Early evening. Last light of the sun. The food stalls are a mess of dirty plates and pots. Puddles of spinach, aubergines and potatoes.

Sometimes Magda wants to walk to the edge of the world and keep walking. Wants to step out of everything and leave it shining in a heap behind her.

She shoves through crowds. Wants to kick, shout, push people into the dust. She stands at a stall. Forgets what she wants. Buys chocolate. It tastes of soap.

Want halva?

The stall holder pushes a sticky cream-coloured ball towards her, wraps it in brown paper.

Best, he says. Go on, take it.

Magda holds the sweet in her hands, heavy as a rock.

There, he says. You will feel good now.

Magda starts to cry. There in the street, amidst the melons and olives, the donkeys and painted pots. People step around her. Let her be. She wipes her hand across her face, runs back to her room.

Magda tells Somah: I used to be twenty. I used to wake in the morning and brush my hair. Eat breakfast. Fill the day with doing. I did things. Those things meant something. I was alive. I knew that.

My mother was dead. I knew that. Dead in the same hour I was born. She had green eyes. I was told that. Yellow hair, green eyes and a mouth like a big red flower. My father said: you are not like your mother, and although I did not know her I knew he spoke the truth.

I was not like her and I was not like him. I was like me. But what was that? It was like being given a tiny corner of a map and being told: that is where you are going. No page number, no reference to any major city or country, no name of street or road. This is where you are going.

And I did not know that place would be here. And I did not know so many things would be missing from me. Old things, new things, things I never had, things I had and watched disappear.

Magda is falling away from herself. Dropping off the end of the world.

Magda says: don't touch me. My skin is made of paper and you may put your fingers through. Then there will be no barriers between your body and mine and you will think my thoughts and dream my dreams until, lost, you will try to find your way back to yourself and discover it is no longer possible.

Magda says: the air in the room is thick and warm. The walls shrink and grow as if they are breathing.

Somah says: we are going to walk. You will feel good on the hill and we will watch the sun.

I can't.

You can.

It's hard to breathe. My body is spinning.

They step towards the door.

Somah says: hold tight to my hand.

Magda does not feel like a real person. A cardboard cut-out. A fake.

Other people know how to live, she says. I learn only by watching them.

Somah says: walk.

I am always somewhere else, looking down on my body.

Walk.

Magda watches Somah's legs moving, right forward down, left forward down. Like machinery. Wills herself to copy. Careful, exact, until she can feel her legs and they ache.

Top of the hill, watching the sun fall heavily into the lake and then vanish. Feet on rocks. Body slow again. Hers. Magda sees the sky, feels the evening wind.

14. Sheboy

Magda tells Somah: they were on the move for years. Magda and her mother. Leaving things behind, consoling themselves with the thought they would replace them.

Moving. Always moving. Faces changed. Landscapes. Temperatures. Hotel rooms with hand basins and small squares of towel. Beds a hundred people had slept in. Worn-thin sheets. Pillows lumpy with dreams.

Magda learned her lessons on buses and trains. Sitting in waiting rooms, poring over books, noting facts on lined paper. Her mother read her work.

Good, she said, good. Now write me a story in which nothing is true.

One night when the hotel room was too small and the headlights of passing cars flashed on their walls like Belisha beacons, they went to a bar. Magda sat at a table enjoying the sensation of the room blurring. Two men playing guitars. A woman with a voice that crawled along her back, sat inside her head, left no room for anything else.

The music made Magda feel warm in her legs. She took off her jumper. Let her head roll back on to the velvet-covered wall. Her mother was dancing. Alone in the centre of the room. Eyes closed. Swaying. Her arms like snakes or the branches of trees.

You want to dance?

The man's face was long. Shy eyes. Held his hand out to Magda. Saw him blur and tremble. The light was red and haloed around him. Didn't want his hand. Just him, standing beside her. Tall man in a creased white shirt.

Magda danced that night. With her mother. In a red room. The singer's voice climbed the walls. The room emptied, filled again, emptied.

Magda was drunk on music, the late hour and the feeling of her body inseparable from everything around her. Walking back, the bite of the air against her closed eyes. Head on her mother's shoulder. One leg in front of the other.

Her mother's voice: can you carry her?

Being hauled up. The man's shoulders. Then the dream: Magda on a horse and she had to hold on tight or she would be thrown off.

Magda says: his voice was the first thing Magda heard as she opened her eyes and caught at fragments of the night before. His voice. The red lights. His voice. The singer's tinselly dress. His voice.

Magda says: this is the story he told:

I was born into the wrong body. Knew it by the time they were squeezing me into rough grey shorts and packing me off to school. I wanted to sit on the wall with the girls, swinging my legs and twisting my hair, not skulk behind the shed playing conkers and spit fights.

My best friend's hair was the colour of wheat. He sat on my bunk late one night, eating toffees.

You're not like us, are you?

No.

You're like a girl, he said.

Yes, I said. Like a girl.

That night I dreamed my shoes were patent leather. I had a dressing table, a music box and a gold and opal ring. Woke to taunts of Sheboy. My best friend whiter than the sheet he hid under.

Sheboy, Sheboy, Sheboy.

The dormitory was crammed with faces. They dressed me up in sheets. Rubbed jam on my face, tied shoelaces in my hair.

Sheboy wiggle, they said.

It felt good. Shameful, but good to wiggle among them, hands on hips, long curtain of hair over one eye.

Got expelled for stealing the Matron's earrings. Small drop diamonds. Liked the way they glinted in her hair, wanted to see how they looked on me.

My mother said I was a disgrace. My father cleared his throat. Told me in his study that some things were best kept secret. Each man, he said, hides the thing he loves – or is it loves the thing he hides? No matter. He told me secrets make intolerable lives tolerable and tolerable lives spicy.

But don't get caught, he said.

He gave me ten pounds. I bought a white lace slip and two shades of lipstick – plum and tangerine. I wore them in my bedroom and then, because they felt so good, I wore them in the hall, the bathroom and the kitchen.

My mother came home early from work, saw me sitting at the kitchen table in lipstick and lace, dropped the box of glasses she was carrying and told me to leave her house.

My father said: the boy stays.

My mother said: then I'll go.

My father said: okay.

A week later, my father moved his lover in to the basement. Leonara. A skinny woman with charcoal eyes. She never said anything but yes.

You like this? You want this? Can I? Will you? Shall we?

Yes.

The yes had different meanings but no one took the trouble to decipher them.

Leonara hennaed my hair until it shone like copper. She let me wear her shoes; my wide toes encased in soft green suede. I loved the click of my unsteady heels on the linoleum floor.

Because Leonara did not speak, I told her things. I uncoiled in front of her, spoke words for the pleasure of tasting them, letting them sit between us like hovering motes of dust.

My father pretended he saw nothing. Locked me out of the basement. Told me he and Leonara weren't to be disturbed. I heard yes, yes, yes through the living room floor.

I watched old black and white movies on the television. Imagined I was Lana Turner, Ginger Rogers, Greer Garson. Whoever looked the prettiest, the happiest, that was who I pretended to be. I lost my edges easily. Blurred and blended like smoke. Slept in Leonara's perfume, wood-scented wrist pressed to my nose.

Met my first girlfriend when I was nineteen. The daughter of the man my father worked for.

Time you were seen out with a girl, my father said.

Henrietta. Mouth like a line on a sheet of paper. Eyes so close together she saw nothing but herself and that was in duplicate. Me, me, I, I. All I had to do was listen.

She liked me. Said I had qualities that were rare in a man. Putting her hand on my arm in her father's silver Mercedes. Smells of leather, lilac air freshener, the cigarette smoke she blew in my face.

Most men don't know how to listen, she said. I looked away from her mouth, cherry lipstick bleeding into the face powder around it. Or kiss, she said. Kiss me.

It was better than I expected. Sweeter. Cooler. I pretended I was Katharine Hepburn.

Henrietta was Spencer Tracy.

She rang two days later. Asked why I hadn't called. Asked if I liked her.

Yes, I said.

Yes? she said. Is that all you can say?

I thought back to the movies. You're beautiful, I said.

I heard her blow out a lungful of smoke.

Beautiful, she said. You really think so?

We went to a movie and she talked through it. I kissed her to make her quiet.

I love you, she said.

To prove it, I asked her to buy me a ring. She chose a chunky gold band. I chose one with an opal stone. Standing in the shop, the assistant shifting his weight from one foot to the other.

It's a woman's ring, Henrietta hissed.

So?

She looked at me and I looked at her and there was no way I was going to look away.

Whatever you want, she said.

And so it was. Step by step.

I wore her underwear – tiny frills of lace and wire – her dresses (not my taste exactly, too modest, but the lightness of them against my skin), body lotions, perfumes, brushes, powders and pastes that brought my face alive. I was prettier than Henrietta. It choked her.

Marriage. It was what everyone wanted for us. Henrietta in white. Me in shades of grey. I said no a hundred times, but the words never left my mouth.

Guest lists, table plans, bridesmaids, flowers, menus. A litany in my head. I woke sweating. My heart banged against the sides of my body. I punched Henrietta in my sleep, put my hands around her throat.

I went to see my father. He was in the basement. I waited for him in the lounge. Looked at the plates on the walls, the prints in gilt frames, the bone-china figures.

My father appeared. Red-faced. But his shirt was tucked in and the middle button of his navy jacket was securely fastened.

Son.

Father. I can't.

You can, he said. Secrets require subterfuge.

I thought of Henrietta's hot little body under mine. Wriggling and clawing.

I love you.

Her cries like fists in my fantasies.

Be quiet.

The tears. Her hunching back.

It was all arranged. Ceremony, honeymoon, house with a garden. Under my striped suit, peach satin and cologne. But it wasn't enough. Saw Henrietta through veils, mouth like the zip of a purse. Heard the boom of the organ, the shuffling of chairs, the shifting and rustling of all those dresses and hats.

I ran. Out of the church, down the road, onto a bus filled with Saturday morning shoppers.

On the bus I met Carmela. I squeezed in next to her. Half my bottom hung off the seat.

Excuse me, I said, would you mind moving your bag?

Yes, she said, moving it a fraction. I would.

Dark green eyes. Black hair. White skin. She took in my starched suit, my greased hair, my out-of-the-packet shirt.

You going to a wedding? she asked, or a funeral?

I'm on the run, I said, from both.

Ended up sitting in a café with her, telling her the lot. She was interested, but no fuss, no questions. Just sat there, chain smoking, sipping Lapsang tea and leaving the scarlet print of her lips on the rim of the cup.

Carmela. The woman I ached to be. Crossing and uncrossing her long legs, a backless mule balancing on the tip of her foot. I wanted to bottle everything she had. Study it again and again, like a great painting. When you are in the presence of perfection, you see the imperfections and they are all part of it. Intrinsically, vitally.

Carmela looked at her watch, sighed, drained the dregs of her tea.

Thank you, she said.

I watched her reapply her lipstick. She reached for her bag.

Take me with you.

What?

Light slanted through the open window but she seemed to be looking at me through a fog.

I can't go back, I said, and I have nowhere else to go.

She stood slowly, purposefully, shaking off the fog like a heavy coat.

I said: can I come with you?

She didn't say yes and she didn't say no. So I followed her in and out of shops. She tried on clothes, bought shampoo, a long rope of blue glass beads. I followed her through a market where dusty mirrors jostled for space with watermelons, cut flowers and bargain bins.

It was a long summer. Sleeping on Carmela's too-short sofa. Waking with the first light. Taking her breakfast: a boiled egg, orange juice, marmalade and toast. Fetching the newspaper, ironing clothes, keeping her flat clean.

I watched her as you might watch an exotic bird resting in a tree outside your window.

You've got me wrong, she said.

No, I said.

I wanted to be so close to her that we merged, making me more like her than like myself.

I am all shadow in the darkness, she said. A silhouette on a moving wall.

I gripped her by the arms but she disappeared. All that was left in my hands were the sleeves of her sweat shirt.

Got to feeling like a monster. Looked at myself in the bathroom mirror and wanted to keep the razor going from my chin through the curls on my chest and down.

One day she told me. Monotone voice, picking holes in her tights. She didn't look at me. Just spoke like it was something she'd read in a book and the central character was someone she knew.

Said her father liked to pretend she was his wife. Said he was still inside her. He had her body and all she had left was her mind, chipping and splintering and peeling away.

Carmela said: secrets rot you from the inside out. They make a hole in you and sometimes the hole is so deep and so wide, there is nothing around the sides of it. Just hole, she said.

It was then I knew she was inside of me. Like her father was inside of her. Like God knows who was inside him and making him do the things he did.

I heard my father's words: don't get caught.

I bought myself a cerise pink wig, a feather jacket, a pencil skirt that crushed my thighs and knees together. Got dressed in the men's toilet under the bridge; went into the ladies and painted my face. That day I walked through a hundred eyes and mouths. I walked through the streets and carried on walking.

15. Part woman, part snake

Magda says: Sheboy told good stories. Sitting in the backs of buses, jolting over pot holes, heads rattling against roofs. He spoke of Carmela, of longing, of getting what you want and finding it isn't what you want after all.

There was a hotel room with cockroaches under the bed. He called them Benny and Eric. Raced them across the floor. Place your bets. Used his winnings to buy Magda an ice lolly. Cherry and vanilla fizz. Watched her eat it.

Magda says: every place was different and the same.

They changed their clothes when they grew tired of them.

Magda's few favourite things in a biscuit tin: shells, stones, an old watch, two feathers, a chocolate wrapper that was gold on one side, silver and pink on the other. Held it up to the sun and let it flare. Like a piece of fire.

Magda says: late at night. Magda's mother and Sheboy talking. Magda slept on a lumpy bed. Fidgeted and wriggled, caught corners of their talk. Striped sheet, bobbled and patched. A jumper over her pillow so she could feel something soft against her face.

Or: Magda's head in her mother's lap on overnight journeys where sleep came and went like mini explosions. Cigarette smoke and steam rising off polystyrene cups of dark-coloured tea. Snatches of dreams and half views of stars and deserts. Her mother's hand in her hair.

Magda says: early morning sun. Everything was yellow: buildings, street, cars. They climbed off a bus and walked about, stretched their aching arms and legs. The tinkle sound of a van parading the streets.

Found rooms with views of the mountains. Jagged spikes trying to pierce the sun. The walls were covered in tiny cream and blue flowers. A stranger's lampshades, china vases, smeary glass clock. The low wooden table was mapped with stains. A woman had scratched her name into the wallpaper by the window: Lucy. Magda imagined her sitting in the buff-coloured rocker, looking out, wanting to let people know she had seen the pale blue mountains leading on and on.

It felt good to take their boots off, unpack their bags, lay out T-shirts, jumpers, trousers on the dark wood shelves. Books, photographs, a red wool rug, Magda's battered biscuit tin.

Magda's mother made tea using the sachets and powders the landlady had provided. Sweet and hot. Soft digestive biscuits, an apple cut into three.

Magda's mother lay full out on one of the beds, hands behind head, muddy shoes dangling off the end. Ran her fingers along the curtain, watched the dust jump then settle in the room.

I like it here, she said.

Magda says: Magda had a mother, a biscuit tin of treasures, memories of a boy with a penchant for crabs. Had made love with a chef on a kitchen floor. Called a rich man father, scratched his sister's off-white face. Now she and her mother had a friend, a set of rented rooms and the possibility of staying still for more than a week. Magda wanted to breathe all the air out of her lungs, feel them collapse into her body like folding beach chairs.

Magda says: Sheboy went out. Came back with pasta, oil, spices in crushed bags.

Don't disturb me, he said. Don't touch that. Taste this.

Hot metal spoon in Magda's mouth. Tongue tastes of paprika and black pepper. She sneezed.

Do you like it?

Yes.

Does it need anything more?

I don't think so.

Magda says: Magda and her mother on the sagging green sofa, its swirling pattern looping Magda's fingers endlessly up and around and down. They watched a movie. Magda's mother standing on a chair waving the aerial at the window.

Is the picture back yet?

Yes, but we've lost the sound.

Magda says: after three days, Magda's mother said: I want to do things with my life.

She said: I want to be somebody.

She said: I want it all to have a purpose, all I've been through, all that I am.

She bought clay and moulded it into a huge figure, part woman, part snake. She was up all night, building.

She said: this will say what I need to say. Everyone who looks at it will know.

Know what?

What is inside me.

The figure loomed. It stretched and sprawled, hissed and curled. In the yellow light, it looked like an enormous rock.

I love it, she said. Isn't it fantastic?

They walked around it. Magda's mother was pink and hot.

Do you really like it?

Yes.

What does it say to you?

Magda looked at the window, said: I'm not very good at this.

Does it say life?

Yes.

Joy and pain. Together. Like lovers at a banquet?

I guess.

And you really like it?

Yes.

Magda's mother slept for a day and a half, then walked into the lounge where the snakewoman stood.

There's more, she said.

Magda says: Magda's mother bought tubes of paint, brushes and canvases the size of rooms. She painted with her fingers, her arms, bits of tree bark and shells.

Don't disturb me, she said. I feel inspired, she said. It is happening. I am painting from my bones.

In the kitchen, scrubbing paint off her arms. The water in the sink was a murky shade of blue. And she was shining.

They looked at the canvas as the sun rose.

Well?

It's good, Magda said.

Magda says: and then: a dancer.

Magda's mother stood at the top of the stairs in footless tights and a turquoise leotard. She pointed her toes. Stretched her arms. Rolled her shoulders.

Magda put the needle on the record and as the notes travelled from the floor into her body and out through her fingers, Magda's mother spun across the hall.

My body is filled with music, she said. There is nothing but the way it makes me feel. Fear like ripped paper, she said, a sadness like ice under green glass.

Her hair flew around her.

I am a dancer, she said.

She was sweating. Wiping her face and back with a towel.

That dance was everything I am.

Magda says: Magda's mother slept. Hair in soft rollers. White cream smoothed across her cheeks and chin.

Magda's bed creaked and slumped in the middle so that

sometimes she woke with her legs higher than her head. And with a line of small red bites burning up the side of her body.

The carpets were sticky. Every plate was chipped and cracked.

Magda's mother liked it.

The sense, she said, of other people's lives. Like a secret history.

Sheboy looked no more convinced than Magda, standing in the kitchen doorway, big hands dangling by his sides.

16. Clockwoman's story

Because there are no seagulls here, the sky hangs like a sheet and flaps into the sea which answers with a hiss over pebbles. Answers with a curl up and up and never reaching smashes down and away to foamy nothing.

There are fish in the shallow waves. Green and silver quivers, showing bellies and the quick slime flash of tails. Magda stands in the sea, skirt hitched up around her thighs and she splashes and grabs. She believes if she holds a sea creature in her hands, she can start over again. Pimpled legs, salty hands, sharp wet spikes of hair.

On the beach, a round white woman sits in layered skirts, petticoats and blouse upon blouse. She is dripping in the sun, her face blotched and wet. Dark hair flops around her face in curtains. In her hands she holds a clock.

Twelve fifteen, says the clockwoman. Hours to go.

And then?

I have to look for my son. He is missing.

Missing?

I told him to take a coat. I knew it was going to rain. I waited and when he didn't come home, I put on my coat and went looking for him. Knew I wouldn't find him but that didn't stop me looking. I told him to take a coat, she says, I knew that it would rain.

Magda sits beside her, hot sand searing through her dress.

How long have you been here? asks Magda.

The clockwoman traces the outline of her clock.

Weeks? asks Magda. Years?

I know that once I was young and my skin was white. I was a singer and my voice filled halls. People gave me flowers. Do you believe me?

Yes, says Magda.

Men were in love with me. They queued outside my dressing room door. Dinner, theatre, cocktail lounges. I walked along the Embankment under the moon. I wanted.

Wanted?

My son is missing. I told him to take a coat. I wanted a son. Wanted one place, one man, one life. I was sick of the stage and the crowds. And the way they made me feel. Over-full but empty. I married my husband because he had soap-coloured eyes and he said he wanted a child.

I've lost it all. I couldn't hold on to it. After a year we found out my husband's sperm were dead. I should have learned not to hope, learned to think about something else. But it was impossible.

The clockwoman says: one night I went to a bar to get numb. I met four men there, lazy and hot on beer. Round the back up against a van with Lilley's Catering across the side. I let them take turns. Dan, Don, Mark and Jake.

I kept hold of my beer the whole time. Remember the warm drip down my arm. The puddle in my elbow, the stickiness under the Cartier watch my husband bought me.

Dan was heavy, bruising. Looked me in the eye the whole time and called me Susan. Susansusiesue. A mantra. He was tight around the belly, like a drum.

Then Don. Bigger than any man has a right to be, but gentle. Kind of man who asks: may I? first and keeps on saying: is that all right? all the way to the end.

And Mark. A boy really. A thin Greek boy with a body like silk. No words or wrong moves. A long time he was inside me. Held him there with the bottle against the small of his back. He was smooth. All ease and flow, like the first cup of coffee in the morning.

Then Jake. Ears like handles, nose like a rock. Coming at me with the force of a steam train. It didn't hurt.

I finished my beer. Had a wash in the toilet. Splashed my face and under my dress, then brushed my hair and went home. I knew my son was inside me.

The clockwoman says: for nine months, my husband thought he'd beaten nature and the doctors but I knew the baby was Mark's before it came out; long and quiet, the colour of a cinnamon stick. My husband stood by the bed, looking into the blankets, searching for a likeness.

He said I'd made a fool of him. Taken him for a bumpy ride. I cried when he left, hadn't planned on bringing up a child alone. Missed him more than I thought I would. But I didn't miss singing or applause because my son was the joy in my life.

The clockwoman curls, breasts against her knees, one hand clamped between her thighs. She closes her eyes.

Everything is blue, she says. The tears roll with no warning. Twelve thirty. Do you think I'll find him? Do you think I'll see my son again? If I don't give up?

Yes, says Magda. I'm sure you will.

The clockwoman lets go of her clock and puts a hand on Magda's hand.

My son's name is Michael, she says. Talk to me when you're passing. I like the colour of your hair.

Magda walks to a stall. She buys a loaf of bread and a bar of chocolate. She always goes to the same stall, they know her, they don't watch her any more. Sometimes she steals a Biro or metal toy.

Afterwards she lines her booty in a row. Although she travels light, Magda likes to hoard. It makes her feel she can stay, makes her feel moving on is a choice.

Sitting by the window in her room, Magda empties her handbag, checking: keys, purse, travellers cheques, passport, earrings, keyspursetravellerscheques. Her purse? Still there. Keys? Yes, she can feel them in her hand. She takes them out, looks at them, says: I have my keys. Puts them back in the bag, zips it shut. Thinks: have I got my keys?

She cannot rest.

The tick of her watch as the seconds fall away. She imagines she can catch them, one by one, dropping off the end of her wrist. Catch them before they disappear.

17. Salt

Magda tells Somah: Sheboy and Magda went for a walk. Found a small port with two old boats. Threw stones into the water. Sat in silence, watching the brown ripples, feeling the sun on the backs of their necks.

Walking back slowly, kicking the dust, Magda's skin felt gritty. And she felt Sheboy pull away, gently. A gap was widening between them, even as they walked side by side, knocking against each other, the collision of arms, a leg against a leg.

I have to move on, he said.

Magda felt something heavy and hard in her chest. She wanted to push him into the water, hold onto him so tight she left marks on his skin.

Why?

This place is not right for me.

And what about me?

What about you?

Don't you care?

Of course I do.

Blood was thumping in Magda's head. So loud he must be able to hear. Her cheeks burned, and her head, her hands.

Magda ran. Could hear him running behind her. Their feet pounding the stones which shifted and rattled. Magda's legs felt like machine parts, connected in a rhythm. She couldn't stop them even if she wanted to.

She looked over her shoulder and he was still running to keep up with her. Magda felt a surge of something hot inside her body.

Wait.

Sheboy was running after her. She mattered enough to him for that.

Blurs of green and blue and brown. A woman with a basket of yellow melons. A man in braces with a beaten-up straw hat.

Magda and Sheboy collapsed in a doorway. Breath loud. Bodies heaving. Sweat dripped from his hair onto her arm and because he was not looking at her – but looking down at the ground, his head on his knees – she licked it. The hot salty flavour of him disappearing in her mouth.

He looked up at last, his eyes hooking hers and she felt herself burning. His body shutting out everything else.

When he pulled back and there was air between them, sharp and cool, her arms went up around his neck. Of their own accord. Drew him back. Held him there against her like a child or a sheltering tree.

It grew dark. They slumped in the doorway, a knot of arms and legs. Wet hair cold against their skin. They had not spoken and of all the words that crammed her head now, only two made their way into the space between them:

at last.

What do you mean?

His voice was quieter than she'd ever heard it.

I don't know, she said. Just that suddenly I feel as if I have been waiting for this.

Magda says: they didn't want to go back. Found an empty bar with dim lights and a waitress peeling her nail polish off in strips, lining them up in a glass ashtray.

Yes?

Magda drank wine, ate pink crab sticks and white rolls, skinny chips and fruit salad. Ate with one hand, the other locked into his under the table.

Magda says: Magda woke folded up in the middle of the bed, like a deck chair. Stretched. Remembered the night before. Lying in the lumpy rented bed, smiling, curling and uncurling her toes. Six fifteen in the morning. Grey sky turning white.

Put on a sweatshirt and thick socks. Padded into the lounge. Saw Sheboy standing by the window, smoking a cigarette. Crept up behind him. Lost inside himself, he did not notice Magda until her hand was inside his.

Magda.

Face so full of smile her cheeks felt huge.

Go back to bed.

Why?

Pulling on his hand, trying to squeeze life into his fingers.

It's wrong Magda.

Wrong?

I'm thirty years older than you.

So?

Felt the beginnings of tears. Behind her eyes, in the back of her throat.

I'm going away, he said.

Quiet. So quiet it was easy to pretend she had not heard him.

It's for the best.

Whose best?

He shrugged and Magda's fingers slipped out of his. Big hands dangling.

You'll forget me.

Magda went on standing next to him, feeling the heat of his body, the chill now of hers.

Go back to bed.

And when I wake, you'll be gone.

More shrugging. He looked like someone had taken a rubber and begun to wipe him out. Fuzzy at the edges.

She didn't want to be whispering. Standing close but miles away from him.

She said: tell me you love me and I'll come with you.

No.

No?

I can't tell you that.

Magda watched the sun pink the sky. A slow blush, yet so soon it seemed there was nothing but red. Watching him leave. Red bleeding into orange.

18. Love potion

Wind whirls in the tops of the trees and searches through the rubbish lining the roads.

The tap at Magda's door is gentle.

Somah, is that you?

No.

Who is it?

Please let me in.

Magda walks to the door. The beach hut is chaotic – used tissues, empty food wrappers, pieces of scribbled-on paper, clothes and cosmetics tumbling out of drawers and all over the floor. She does not want a stranger inside her room.

She opens the door slightly, puts her head out, sees a woman dressed in black.

Quickly, let me in.

The woman squeezes through the gap in the door,

shrinking and stretching like a tom cat. Sits on the edge of the bed, slips her feet out of sandals.

Says: I am Reeta. Somah told me about you. I need you to help me.

Help you?

My husband Marius. Have you met him?

Yes.

He likes foreign women. He thinks of nothing else.

Reeta says: I married Marius when I was seventeen. He was handsome. He smiled with his teeth. Gave me flowers. He was a good husband. Never hit me. Never laughed at me. Didn't get drunk too much. The other women saw him. I knew their talk. But I had him. I was happy.

Magda sits opposite Reeta on the bed.

When we had been married less than a year, Marius's uncle in England sent him money for an aeroplane ticket. One ticket. I asked him not to leave me. But he did not listen. The time he was gone was worse than I could have thought. It was as if my belly went with him. Stretched across the sea. I could not eat or sleep or work.

I wrote him letters. Four or five a week, begging him to come home. He stayed away two years. Found work in England. A new name. Women. He did not want to come back but his uncle made him. Said it was time to be with me, start a family.

When he came back he was different. Hard and wooden. His eyes were somewhere else. He said he was in love with a woman he met for one night only. He didn't know her name. I tried everything but he was gone from me.

My mother-in-law said it was my fault. I did not know what do to. I asked what would make him happy and he said a divorce. The one thing I would refuse him. I said no. He said he didn't need me to say yes, but he would accept my wishes. He was a dull man then, empty of feelings.

After that he kept asking, a divorce, a divorce. I said no. And no again. Then I went to my room.

Reeta says: the tears are dammed up behind my eyes and sit in my chest. I would scream but I am hemmed in on all sides. No way for anything to escape. I am an egg that will never crack.

I say no by lying on cushions and eating tiny mouthfuls. People notice that. They say: she is sick, because they can see it. They want to help. My power lies in the fact they can do nothing for me.

Magda asks: what do you want me to do?

Give me a potion to make him love me.

I have no potion.

What about English woman's smell.

My perfume?

Something you have that I don't. I need to know what English women know.

Magda rummages through a stack of damp T-shirts and finds a bottle of cologne.

You can have this, she says. But it won't work.

19. Sugar

The clockwoman is in her usual place. Legs spread wide.

Hello, says Magda.

Eleven fifteen.

Would you like a drink?

If I move I might miss my son.

From the roof of that bar, Magda says, you might be able to see him more clearly.

The clockwoman stands like a small mountain. Leaves a puddle on the sand. Rolls rather than walks. Grunts more than she breathes.

The stairs up to the roof have her puffing and wheezing, pausing mid-step to bury her head in her sleeve.

The greasy-faced owner is dozing in a chair. Magda asks

for two cups of coffee and, without opening his eyes, he clicks his fingers. A boy appears at the door to the kitchen, wiping his hands along his shorts.

Two coffees, says the owner.

The boy disappears.

The table is sticky with spilt coffee and crumbs. Sleepy flies sit in the sugar bowl. A brown beetle with several legs missing crawls lop-sidedly towards them.

The clockwoman says: I shall describe my son for you. In case you see him and I'm not around. He looks a lot like me. And a lot like his father. Tall and wiry. His eyes are brown. His skin as smooth as an apple.

Magda asks: do you have a photograph?

The clockwoman puts her hand inside her blouse and brings out a creased black and white picture of a boy playing with a toy giraffe.

How old was your son when he disappeared?

Nineteen, says the clockwoman. The same age as his father when I met him.

The coffee is lukewarm and very sweet. Magda watches the clockwoman stir six extra spoonfuls of sugar into her cup. She takes small sips with her fingers curled and crooked. Wipes her mouth on her sleeve.

The clockwoman says: he went to find his father. Said I was spoiling him. Too much love and not enough air. As if that explained everything. He sold his record player, his watch and the fine gold chain I bought him for his sixteenth birthday.

I offered him all the money I had in my purse and he stuffed it into his back pocket. I asked him not to leave but that just made him more determined. I stood in front of the door and he pushed me away and into the wall.

Don't know when you'll hear from me again, he said. Get on with your life, he said. Remember me when there are storms, when the trees ache to split and the sky is a giant patchwork. That's when I'll think of you.

The clockwoman rolls a grain of sugar between her thumb and forefinger.

I remember him every hour of every day, she says. You can't imagine the pain of losing your child. It is like having your insides ripped out and then stuffed back in. Afterwards, nothing is ever right again.

No, says Magda.

20. Floating island

Magda walks to the roof-top bar. Sees the village moving beneath her, takes a book from her bag.

Marius is sitting a few tables away. He leans back and finishes his coffee, motions for a refill.

Hello, he calls.

He takes a long drink, fiddles with the cup, wipes his lips with his sleeve.

I made a mistake with you.

Yes. It doesn't matter.

It does matter. The honour of my family. I am a respected man. I run a chain of clothing shops in the city. I have money. I will buy you coffee.

No thank you.

One coffee.

No.

I want to be your friend.

I don't need a friend.

Marius walks around chairs and tables to get to her. Sits at her table, flicking his cigarette into the ashtray.

Magda says: please leave.

Give me one chance.

He smiles and she can see orange stains between his teeth.

Please.

Marius says: I can show you places. A floating island, a cave filled with crystals. I am an excellent guide.

Magda says: no thank you, looking up from her book, shielding her eyes from the glare of the sun.

He is wearing white trousers with a drawstring waist, a powder blue shirt and shoes with a small stacked heel. His hair and moustache are oiled.

You are frightened, he says. Always with your head in a book.

That's how I like it, Magda says, but she closes her book.

Magda pays for her drink, packs her book into her rucksack, follows Marius down the stone steps and out onto the street.

This way, he says.

His fingers touch her elbow to steer her. She steps

aside but follows him through the town. Narrow dirty lanes.

Marius and Magda clamber into a taxi, jolt over rocks. Marius falls against Magda, says: you have no reason to feel afraid.

I'm not afraid.

Then why are your shoulders up by your ears?

Magda folds her arms across her chest.

You watch me too much, she says.

He lights a cigarette, flicking the match on to the floor. Leans back and his leg is against hers all the way from hip to knee.

The taxi stops at the edge of a cliff. The air is still. A dog with three legs licks a sore on his back.

At Magda's feet, there is a tiny pile of bleached bird skeletons. She moves closer towards the edge. Curls her toes over, stands looking down to the bottom.

Marius' hand is on her waist. The ground bumpy and falling away.

What are you doing?

I want to look.

He releases his grip, lets her move back with him.

I'll have to keep watching you, he says.

They climb down to the lake. Pebbles crumble under their

feet. Magda clutches at the long grasses, grazes her palms. Marius holds out his hand.

Let me help you.

I can manage.

He is laughing at her. From behind, she sees his shoulders move, hears a rough sound in his throat. She is hot and tired. She takes his hand because it is better than falling. His gold ring is smooth, his fingers no bigger than her own.

The lake is bordered by spindly trees. The water is a tangle of green weeds. Smells of urine and decay.

Magda asks: where is the floating island?

Marius says: it's not always possible to see it.

Magda scratches an insect bite on her ankle. Says: then why are we here?

Because today might be the day it appears.

Magda turns her back towards him, searches for a bottle of water in her rucksack.

Marius finds a cigarette in his pocket and lights it with one hand; the other is digging a small hole in the ground.

They keep looking at the lake, but neither expects to see anything. They skim stones, watch a bird circle the water over and over.

Magda asks: have you brought Reeta here?

No.

He starts digging a second hole with his heel. Dust flies.

Why not?

Because Reeta doesn't believe in anything she can't touch.

A slow breeze begins, ripples the water, plays with the front strands of Magda's hair.

Marius says: I left Greece once. Lived in London with my uncle. Worked on a building site. Saw another world.

I met a woman in England. Several women. But one special woman. She was alone in a bar drinking beer and eating olives. I watched her eat around the stones. She was not looking for anyone.

Her dress was covered in small red berries. She was wearing plimsolls and black woollen tights. Her hair was scraped back off her face in a wide black band. And I couldn't talk to her. Not a word. Standing beside her at the high wooden bar. I was with the men I worked with. Three of them. They noticed her too, of course. Made jokes, kept trying to get her attention.

Our backs and shoulders ached. The jukebox played Cliff Richard's Living Doll over and over until I wanted to pull the plug out of the wall.

Marius says: it was early evening. There was no one else in the bar. We were just getting ready to leave when she started talking. Flirting talk. She rolled her eyes, scratched at a small hole in the knee of her tights. I knew it wasn't real. Not her. Not what I'd seen anyway.

I can't remember how it happened, but we all ended up out in the car park. And she was available. To all of us. Didn't even put down her beer. One after the other.

But there was something between her and me. Like the roll of a wave just before it crashes. And I couldn't say anything.

Marius stands and walks to the lake, lets the water splash up and over his shoes. Strokes the scummy surface with a reed.

We got wrecked that night. Stopped in at seven or eight bars. Got so loud they threw us out. We were all on a strange high, couldn't believe the way it happened.

Magda's head is stretched so tight she feels it is about to burst.

Was the woman a singer?

I don't know, he says. She didn't even tell us her name.

Was she wearing a Cartier watch?

Yes, he says. Clamped to her left wrist. Fat with silver and diamonds. Why?

If you saw her again, what would you do?

Marius says: that's impossible. I'd have to go back to England and try to find her and I have no information and—

Yes, but if it was possible. Say, if she was here in Greece and you met her on the street. Then what?

I don't know, he says. She changed my life once. She would probably do the same again.

21. Shapes and shadows

Reeta is waiting for Magda in her room.

You saw Marius?

Yes.

You spoke to him?

Yes.

What did he say?

Magda puts down her rucksack. Fiddles with the straps.

Reeta says: I have been waiting for you all day. You must tell me something.

Magda says: he took me to look for the floating island.

And you didn't see it.

No.

Reeta stands, walks to the window.

He lives in dreams, she says. I am worse than a widow. They all talk. I have a husband I can't keep. I used your perfume. He didn't notice. I went close and it was the same as always.

The room feels too small.

Magda says: let's go for a walk.

Outside?

We can go to the market and drink coffee.

Reeta says: it has been a long time since I did that.

Reeta walks slow, close to the walls. Eyes darting. She sees the clockwoman in the shadows.

Says: she is crazy. Says: she has been here for a long time. She is like a man. Always on the street.

Magda says: she is sad, like you.

Reeta says: she is nothing like me.

Walks past, taller.

They sit at the back of a bar where flies are dying slowly.

Reeta asks: is Marius in love with someone else?

Magda says: you need to fill your head with something other than him.

Then he will love me again?

The moon is full and low in the sky. Walking back, Magda looks up and sees its shapes and shadows.

Magda says: look, the moon is many colours tonight.

Reeta says: it just looks like the moon to me.

22. Creased yellow bird

Magda once read a newspaper article about a woman who didn't speak for more than forty years. The doctors could find nothing wrong with her. In her fifty-sixth year, walking down the high street in the fraying yellow anorak no one had ever seen her without, she tripped over a small pile of rubbish. Sprawling on the pavement, she began to cry.

A shop-keeper – the man she had been buying eggs, cheese and bread from for half a century – ran out on to the street in time to hear her say: I told him not to. Later that afternoon, she climbed on to the roof of the library and walked out into the air. Falling, her scream was so loud and so long it sent shivers through the trees.

Trees stand stark against the evening apricot light. Fireflies in the marshes. Spires of smoke.

Magda finds the storyteller at his usual table. Says: I have a story and I don't know whether to tell it or keep it to myself.

Stories are meant to be told, says the storyteller. Otherwise they stay small.

Magda says: if I tell the story I will affect its outcome. But if I don't tell it, I will be getting in its way. It's like playing God.

No not God. A storyteller is only a messenger. Every story, says the storyteller, has a life of its own.

Daylight slants like a razor. Magda fills a metal bin with biscuit wrappers, newspapers and banana skins. She shakes the sheet on the sagging mattress. Puts books in a pile, pens in a pot. Scrapes candle wax off the windowsill. Collects cobwebs with her fingers and rolls them into tiny balls.

At ten thirty-five, the clockwoman arrives.

Am I early?

No, says Magda, you are perfectly on time.

She leads her into the room, offers her a cigarette, a

drink, a chair, says: I think I've found the man you've been looking for.

My son?

No. Magda says: not your son. Your son's father.

Here?

Yes.

The clockwoman picks up her clock and walks towards the door.

I don't want to see him.

Why not?

The clockwoman looks at her ripped yellow dress, the scratched red polish on her toes, the Sellotape around the buckles of her shoes. Says: once I was beautiful. I wore diamonds and men loved me. I danced on tables, sang to packed rooms, slept on the petals of bouquets. But what man would want me now?

Marius walks into the room as if it is his. Notices the clockwoman perched on the bed like a creased yellow bird and says: hello.

The clockwoman says: hello.

They look at each other and they look away.

Magda says: I wanted you two to meet.

The clockwoman asks: why? Says: I see this man most days in the street.

Marius says: sometimes I buy her a coffee. She talks about her son. I get bored. I go away.

No, says Magda. Don't you remember?

Remember?

You met in a bar. You spent thirty-five minutes in each other's company. You totally altered the course of each other's lives.

Marius asks: is this the woman I told you about?

Yes, says Magda, yes.

Then it is over, he says, forever. It is as if the dream never was.

The clockwoman says: he is the man that became of the boy. But it was the boy I loved.

Magda asks: how can you know they are not the same?

The boy was a friend of my heart, she says, this man is a stranger to me.

23. Colours

Midday. A burning, colourless sun.

Magda says: stories change lives.

The storyteller says: that is their purpose.

But what if you make someone's life worse?

Worse? The storyteller shrugs his shoulders. You never know that.

But I do. Magda feels her hands grow hot. I got inside a story and broke people's dreams.

The storyteller's eyes are green with splashes of brown.

You still don't know you have spoiled their lives, he says.

The storyteller tells a story:

there once was a boy who lived with his father in a hut by the sea. One day, walking on the cliffs, he saw a beautiful horse. Nine hands high and white as the moon. He was drawn towards it as a bird to the sky.

The horse stood very still and let the boy stroke it. Then they rode for miles. The boy built a large fence to enclose the horse. He was so happy he felt his stomach would explode.

That night, he sat with his father and said: finding this horse is the most wonderful thing that has ever happened to me. The boy's father lit a cigarette. He took a long time answering.

It could be the most marvellous happening, he said. But it could also be the most painful.

The boy felt his father had poured cold water onto his fire. Blood rushed to his face and banged in his ears. What did his father know? He was an old man; he'd probably never felt this happy in his whole life.

The boy and his white horse spent a blissful summer together. But one day the horse galloped away. The boy ran after him wildly, awkwardly. His lungs stung with gasps. But the horse was too fast and too determined to go.

The boy stayed until the cliffs darkened and shadows began to creep out at him from the trees. His heart was totally broken. He had lost everything that mattered to him. He felt his life was over.

That night he cried to his father, losing my horse is the

worst thing that has ever happened. His father held him tight and took a long time to speak.

It could be the worst happening in your life, he said. But it could also be the most joyful.

The boy was dismayed by his father's words. Didn't his father realise it was impossible for him to feel happy ever again?

For months there were no colours in the boy's life, nothing that made his heart soar. Then one day, off in the distance in the long tangling grasses, he saw a cloud of shimmering whiteness. His whole body filled with excitement. He ran across the fields towards his horse.

The horse was not alone. He had brought a cream-coloured mare with him and a handsome, leggy foal. Together, the four returned to his father's house.

I never would have believed it, the boy told his father that night. When I lost my horse the world turned dark. But now my life is better than ever. Not one white horse, but three. This, surely, is the very best thing that could ever happen.

Again, his father said: best or worst, who knows?

The storyteller says: when you tell a story it becomes part of you and changes you.

The sun is the colour of honey. Smell of damp wheat.

Sky flecked with birds: green, blue, white, black. Magda thinks of Missing, her mother, her pale brown man.

If you change your stories, Magda asks, can you change yourself?

24. No edge

This night, the night that follows her meeting with the storyteller, the night when she is thinking that if she changes her stories, she might be able to change herself, Magda sits with Somah. She is peeling a tangerine. Curls of orange skin. The warm air in the bedroom is spiked with the sharp citric scent.

Magda says: would you like a story?

And when Somah says: yes,

Magda says: Sheboy said: I'm going away. Quiet. So quiet it was easy to pretend Magda had not heard him.

I know this story, says Somah.

No, says Magda, no. It is a different story. Everything is different. You see, Sheboy took Magda with him.

Magda says: this is the way it happened.

And Magda says: Sheboy and Magda left together. Left Magda's mother behind in the rented rooms, with her secret histories, her faulty television and her painting called Rest.

Magda told Sheboy: I wish I could say it is hard to leave, that I worry how my mother will feel, waking to find us both gone, that I am leaving a part of me with her, in gratitude, in love. I am. I'm sure of it. But this morning all I can think of is you and our future.

Left her biscuit tin behind, took only her clothes and her mother's fuchsia lipstick. Crept away, her insides somersaulting over and over. Put her hand inside Sheboy's and felt his hand squeeze hers back.

Blue morning. Streets stirring. Shutters lifting on shops.

Sheboy asked: are you sure?

Yes.

It's not too late to go back.

Do you want me to?

Silence. And still their feet kept moving forward.

Do you want me to go back?

No, he said at last. Not unless you want to.

Magda says: another bus. Windows white with condensation. Magda wiped a clear square. Sheboy beside her. The bus sounded like a lawn mower, rattling and whining around their heads. It lunged forward, so that they fell against the seats in front.

Magda says: they found a room that smelled of wood smoke and damp sheets. A picture of Mary in white over the bed. Stumpy candles melting on windowsills; shapes of frogs and misshapen hands. They sat on the edge of the bed and spoke about the journey, then they spoke about dinner, then they sat in a noisy silence.

He was so close Magda could feel his breath against her hair, but she could not move. Not until his hand was in her hair and at her throat and a thousand sensations thudded through her. Then movement was like swimming in warm water.

His body was the first Magda held under her hands. First hips, first knees, first arms. Lying so close there was no edge, no him, no her. Fluids passing between them, mouth, cunt, penis, like a river with no beginning and no end.

Magda says: Magda woke in sunshine so bright she could not open her eyes. His arm across her, her leg across him. The whistle of a bird that sounded as if it was in the room with them. Sheboy. Lashes sweeping his cheeks. Hair spread out across the pillow like a hundred arms. His arms moving now, pulling her in.

Half-asleep, they rocked together. Slower and more gentle than anything she had known.

Magda says: the first nausea was like a bubble.

Magda thinks: it could have happened this way, could have, should have.

Magda says: Magda ran from the bed to the bathroom. She felt yellow, green. Something was inside her and it wanted to come out. The landlady heard her retching. Poked her head around the door. All patchwork skin and too-big eyes.

Are you pregnant?

What do you mean? Of course I'm not pregnant.

Of course, she said.

Her keys jangled. Her slippers slipped and slopped on the bare wood stairs. Magda pushed her and her words away. Drank a glass of wine in the midday heat. Sitting by the window, looking out through the top branches of trees. Fell asleep and woke sweating. Beads of wine on the carpet. A semi-circle of red.

Sheboy came back with a grilled fish and melon. Laid out a picnic on the bed. Magda was hungry. Ate hugely. Unable to pause between mouthfuls. Not bothering to speak.

After he asked her: how was your morning?

She wanted to tell him, but didn't want the landlady's words in the room with them, so—

I got tipsy and slept, she said.

Good, he said.

He told Magda: I met a man with a boat, in the shop where I was buying our lunch. He's setting sail in the morning. Said we can go with him, if we like.

Magda thought of waves on water. Nothing but blue. A break from bumpy buses, dust and smoke. Said: yes.

Yes, before they met Claude in a bar. Skin-tight jeans and tattoos up his arms, dragons curling around his biceps with flaming tongues. Claude was all gold teeth and whiskers. By the time he leaned across the bar and breathed beer and Gauloise into Magda's face, it was too late. Sheboy was beaming. She thought of her mother in the sagging green room.

Magda says: it happened like this: they set sail early in the morning. The clank of metal chains, ropes whizzing through fists like snakes. Magda shivered on the deck in her summer dress. Water-logged toes. Flies around their heads.

Wanted a blazing sunrise. Not a washed-out pastel sky. Wanted dolphins and whales, not the stench of fish guts and latrines. Leaned over the side of the boat and vomited into the sea.

Claude had only two cups, two plates, two sets of cutlery. Sheboy and Magda passed them back and forth between them. Thin green soup, fried eggs, rum. He kept them up late. Stories of his conquests – naval and female. A lantern banging and throwing light haphazardly, manically.

His high-pitched laugh. The way he clapped his hands together as if the whole world was inside them. Magda's head lolled against the sides of the ship. Smells of damp wood and seaweed.

She wanted only to curl up next to Sheboy. Twelve o'clock, one o'clock, two. They seemed interested only in each other. Tucked her head inside her jumper and slept.

Magda woke early. Felt as if someone had poured oil down the back of her throat. It was inside her mouth, her nose, her ears.

Slept too close to the engine, Claude said.

Eyes ringed red, he looked older than he had the night before.

They had all slept where they were on the deck. Covered by hessian sacks and a blanket that scratched as much as it smelt. Sheboy could barely lift his head.

Not used to rum?

Claude tried to laugh but ended up coughing violently. Throwing his arms around.

Porridge made with water. Five spoons of grey sugar and still it made Magda shudder. Spent the day avoiding Claude. Pretended to sleep rather than catch his eyes. Lost herself in a book. Counted the hours until they docked. Sheboy still inert under sacks.

Magda says: when Claude came up behind Magda in the cramped kitchen and clamped his hands around her waist, she was not surprised. Stirred the hot water in her plastic teacup.

Come on baby, he said. Baby, baby, he said.

Imagined the dragons writhing and twitching. Maybe Claude Loves Mum between the hairs on his chest – or Love, perhaps, and Hate.

No need to tell your friend, he said. Our secret, he said. You and me.

Could feel him hard against the small of her back. Hard and small.

One arm around her waist, hand bundling up her skirt.

Magda said: get off.

What?

His hands did not move.

You heard me.

Come on baby.

Get off me.

What's the problem?

Threw her tea at him. Saw the dark stain spread across the front of his jeans.

Don't touch me, she said.

Fat chance, he said.

Hands at his crotch.

Just being friendly, he said. It's not like you're so great.

Magda says: Sheboy emerged from under the hessian sacks. Dived fully-clothed into the sea. Floated belly up. Limbs like the points of a star. Magda watched him. A white speck in the endless blue. Drifting further and further away.

It was early evening. Her skin was stretched and creased by sun and salt wind. Saw Claude leafing through a pornographic magazine. Flashes of pink skin, black hair, all arches, curves and openings.

Magda jumped. The water bubbled up around her head and she was falling. Falling and being held at the same time. Her body was weightless, suspended, invisible.

Then her ears exploded. Her head was filled with water, blackness, pin-pricks of swirling light. Magda was on the surface again, in the air. Heart thudding and jumping. She lay back on the shifting blue and let it lift and drop her. Like a lover, it moulded to her curves, rippling beneath.

When she began to grow cold, she swam to Sheboy. They clung together in the water, wrapped around each other, holding each other up. There was a silver moon. Tentative stars. They were in a big blue room and wherever they went it grew bigger to accommodate them.

We ought to go back, Sheboy said at last.
She swam behind him all the way.

Magda tells Somah: that night they played cards. Sitting amidst piles of sacks, crisp packets and cigarette ends. Magda sat nearby, read her book, caught enough of their talk to know Sheboy was losing. Badly. Saw him mash his hands together.

Better stop now, he said. Magda and me, we haven't got much and we need it. To eat, he said. Find rooms, he said. Think I'd better call it a night.

Come on, said Claude. He wiped the top of his rum bottle and passed it to Sheboy. Sheboy hesitated, took a small shuddering swig, passed it back.

Give up now and you're a loser. Keep going and you could be a winner. Could end up with more for you and Magda. Make things easier for you, he said, better.

Sheboy rubbed his hands along his legs, then, slowly. He took another handful of notes from his pockets and straightened out the creases. Laid them down in front of him.

All right, he said.

More rum, more cigarettes. The lantern swaying madly. The glint of Claude's gold teeth, mirrors of the lanterns in his eyes.

Magda read the same paragraph three times. Words

were floating, separate things: she, he, they. She read it once more, trying to take in its meaning. Then, because she could not stand it a moment longer, she made herself sleep.

She woke when she punched her hand against the side of the boat. Grazed her knuckles. Wanted to weep.

Sheboy was hunching forward, with his back to her. A map of sweat on his shirt. Claude was grinding a cigarette butt into the deck. They were not looking at each other.

Sheboy stood and stretched, crumpled clothes sticking to him. The night was suddenly silent, almost still.

Magda says: Magda watched Sheboy bend down and begin picking up notes. He did it three times, four, five. Folding them in tidy piles. Then Sheboy scooped them into his pockets – the pockets of his trousers, his shirt, his denim jacket.

He stood there, shrugging at Claude, but Claude would not look at him.

Good night Claude, he said at last.

Claude grunted, eyes fixed on the sea.

Magda says: fifteen hundred pounds, Sheboy could not stop saying it.

Huddled under the blanket with Magda, hands fidgeting at his pockets.

Fifteen hundred pounds, can you believe it? Fifteen hundred pounds. Like taking a bottle from a baby.

You got lucky, Magda said.

Lucky? he said. No, he said. I've been winning at cards since I was twelve.

Magda says: by the time they got to Hydra, Claude was not talking to either of them. Hadn't spoken a word in days. Sheboy and Magda swam, read aloud to each other, played Charades and Snap. Ate their rations of chocolate and pistachio nuts. Stole triangles of cheese and soft biscuits from Claude's larder. They dozed on and off all day and through the night, woke at odd hours to whisper.

Hydra. Five o'clock in the morning. Fishermen in clumps. Torchlights down to the water. A squid thrashing and flipping on the quay. Black ink puddle.

Time to say goodbye, Claude said. His eyes were tiny slits in his face. Saw tobacco between his teeth. The final flash of gold. Clambered onto the quay and felt like laughing. Feet on land, a floor that did not move.

25. Blue

Magda tells Somah: another white-washed room. Wood bed, wood table, two chairs. White darned sheets. Yellow flowers in a honey pot.

This time when Magda was sick, head over the toilet bowl, Sheboy was beside her, his hand on the back of her neck.

He said: are you all right?

Yes.

Has this happened before?

What?

You vomiting in the morning.

What do you mean?

Magda are you pregnant?

No.

He smoothed her hair, the strands caught in her mouth, her damp cheeks.

How do you know?

I just do.

Magda says: they went for a walk. Passed a line of white and terracotta houses. Sprigs of dry green, a goat, a grey dog, two long-eared cats flattened in the shade. Up. Small stones scattering. Trying to get a foothold. Letting him lead.

Up. Her belly felt like a beach ball. Hands in the hollow of her back, pushing upwards. Sweat in rivers on her back, under her arms, collecting around her neck. Mouth hanging open, thick with hot air and too much tongue.

At the top of the hill, the grass grew sparsely, wispy stalks between white rocks, scorched yellow and brown by the sun. Found the bones of a bird, scattered black feathers, a tail ruffling in the breeze like a Flamenco's fan. Magda dug a hole in the rocks with her hands. Buried it all: the bones, the feathers, the tail, lifting it out of a sticky puddle, heavy and sun-warmed in her hands.

Magda says: Magda's baby grew in a flat belly.

She gave her no food.

Still she grew.

Plopped out onto a white and green bath mat. The pain

lasted only a few moments. A low cramp, then the feeling she was being kicked from inside.

Magda called out for Sheboy. But he was not there. Squatted in her own blood and shit, holding a baby she did not want. Hush now hush. The baby cried. Mouth smaller than her fist. Eyes a milky shade of blue. Hush.

Magda didn't want her and yet she was flesh of her flesh, heart of her heart. Held her against her. Felt her heart.

Magda says: Sheboy came back with prawns and aubergines. He didn't move in the doorway, eyes on them. The newspaper package dripped grease on his hands. Magda saw that he wanted to run.

She said: don't.

What?

Leave me.

What do you mean?

Don't leave us.

He walked towards them, stroked Magda's cheek and then the baby's.

Why would I? he said. How could I?

Magda says: in the morning he went to buy oranges and nappies.

Be as quick as I can, he said. Love you, he said.

He kissed them both quickly. She saw him count his

change, take his jacket, look around the room as if he had left something behind.

Magda said: what?

What?

What are you looking for?

Nothing.

Are you sure?

Yes, he said.

He did not come back.

Magda says: they sat by the window, looking out. At first it was a game. Planned to see him coming up the street and call to him, wave. The street was empty for so long, she checked to see her watch had not stopped. Put it to her ear, the tick, tick, tick. Thirty minutes, forty, forty-five.

Told herself he had stopped off for a drink, run into the landlady, run under a car. Paced the room so many times she recognised the shapes of the crumbs on the carpet.

After an hour, she knew. Though she fought against knowing.

After two hours, she thought: Sheboy is gone, I should be crying. But when what you have most feared happens, suddenly, and for a moment, there is nothing to fear.

Magda says: Magda was alone in a hotel room with a baby

she did not want. Her breasts were tight and sore. Hush now hush. It will be all right.

Magda says: Magda did not sleep. Every creak in the hall and on the stairs was Sheboy. He would change his mind. Things could still be all right.

She tried not to let her heart flare with every passing noise. The plummeting was like sea waves wiping out patterns in the sand; it left her with nothing.

Magda says: there was a red bulb in the room, dangling from the ceiling on a piece of grey flex. At night it swung. She watched it for hours. She loved that red light. The way it tinted the shadows, made everything glow.

26. Stealing

Next day. Afternoon collapsing into evening.

Magda is sitting in a bar. She is thinking: if you change your stories you can change yourself. She is watching a bird pick at a half-eaten roll. She is listening to a mother tell her child: you must never do that. Never, ever.

Confusion.

Magda sees a baby in a pram.

Fear.

The mother has run inside a shop and it would be so easy.

Panic. Act now. Before.

The street is too empty, it should not be this easy.

Before.

Legs moving towards the pram and standing by it,
looking in.

The mother is taking too long, it is her own fault.

Magda thinks: come out now and stop me, there is still
time. See my hands are only just on the push bar. It feels
hot. The baby is sleeping in layers of white and it is not
too late. I am moving as slowly as I can. Come out and
stop me.

But Magda's legs are moving faster now and the wheels
are turning. The baby throws a sleepy arm up out of the
whiteness and if she cries now everything will be all right.
It can still be all right.

Up the street and around the corner to a place where
a tree pushes its roots up under the concrete making
the stones uneven. Rest. Look around. Think of pushing
the pram away and down the hill. Her baby now. To
care for.

The thinnest of yellow light falling on a pile of crinkled
leaves. Two teenagers on the corner.

Miss, they call, miss. You got the time?

Ten past four.

Nice baby. They laugh.

They cannot know.

She says: yes.

Got a cigarette?

No, she says, yes.

Stands on the corner with them in the weak light, smoking.

27. Pearl

Train station. Everything covered in dust. People, suitcases, bars, cars. Dust that moves, light as talcum powder.

The man behind the counter wears wire spectacles that make his eyes so big and near Magda finds it hard not to tilt forward to touch them.

Where to?

Because she'd thought only of getting-away-from and not going-to, she stands, mouth open, arms drooping. Dust swirls about her as she shoves a small fist of notes under the partition window and says: south.

A fan creaks over her head. A hanging blanket of cobwebs and dirt.

Magda takes a seat by the window. The train moves down

the hill. Cloud shadows drift over red earth and blue water and the glass, cement and metal town.

The baby cries and a mother rises up in Magda. Hands moving, rustling, cooing sounds, there, there, patting, smoothing, making smooth.

Bundled up in a cardigan, the baby likes to lie on Magda's chest and feel the beat, beat, beat of her heart. And Magda likes to hold her there. Her hair smells of vanilla essence.

Beautiful baby.

Magda nods.

Aren't babies the most wonderful things?

The stranger makes Magda feel she has done something good. Produced something that matters. Something out of nothing.

Where are you going?

It is in that moment, Magda knows. To see my mother, she says.

Does she know she's a grandmother?

A grandmother? No, Magda says, not yet.

Three buses, two boats, nights in hotels with neon signs that buzz in her dreams. One small town after another, like beads on a piece of string.

They arrive around seven in the morning. Magda's head

is heavy. Her mother's rooms seem so far away she thinks of sleeping in the bus shelter. Anything not to move.

The Rooms To Rent sign creaks in the wind. No light in her mother's room. She throws a handful of stones at her window. Please wake up.

Magda.

Her mother's face at the window. Red hair in sponge rollers.

Magda, Magda.

She runs down the stairs and they are in each other's arms. Magda, Magda's mother, Magda's baby.

She presses her lips to Magda's hair. Standing in the deserted street in the light from the porch.

Are you all right?

Magda nods. Face against her mother's night dress, plastic button hard against her cheek.

Still they do not move.

Upstairs, Magda sits on the sagging green sofa. Her mother makes tea: the kettle steams. Round biscuits on a round plate. The baby wrapped up in the armchair, fist outstretched.

Magda's mother pours tea, stirs in sugar, milk, rum. Lays it on the low table in front of Magda, says: where is the father?

I don't know.

You don't know?

No, Magda says. No, I don't know. She hesitates. He went out to buy nappies and he didn't come back.

Magda feels the tears at the back of her throat, sharp and dry.

Magda's mother says: poor baby. She takes Magda's hand in hers, pats her fingers, traces a patch of road dirt with the ball of her thumb. Poor, poor baby.

Magda sits at the little table overlooking the street. Her mother holds the baby on her lap. Studies her face with her fingers.

What's her name?

Name?

Yes, her name, the baby's name. What do you call her?

I don't call her anything.

Nothing?

No.

A baby without a name.

Magda traces the bumps on the wall with the flat of her hand. Plaster crumbles, sits on the tablecloth like chalk dust.

What about calling her Naomi? says her mother. Or Carla?

Magda shrugs.

Or Susan?

Magda hears the swoosh of cars on the wet road. Feels their vibrations running up and down her body.

What about Bethan? says Magda.

Or Riana?

Melanie?

Lesley?

Claire?

Magda calls her daughter Pearl. For all the hidden things.

Her mother reaches for her flask of rum, pours the reddish liquid into two glasses, clinks them together.

Hot as the sun, she says. Burn your insides.

They empty the flask. Bodies like liquid. Sitting by the window, watching the clouds chase the sun.